Coveted Bride

Regina Tittel

The Ozark Durham Series vol. 3

COVETED BRIDE

Published by Hawse Pipe Ministries
Copyright © 2012 by Regina Tittel
Cover design by Regina Tittel

ISBN-10: 0-9889002-3-8
ISBN-13: 978-0-9889002-3-3

Regina Tittel's books are written to uplift and encourage each individual while also entertaining them with a great story. It is the author's prayer that Coveted Bride will reach those who have been or are currently living under emotional abuse and show them how worthy they are.

Were her eyes playing tricks on her?

Lindsey stepped outside and settled Clara on the lawn next to her. She moved the chairs back into place. The toddler kept pace back and forth to the house for the first couple of chairs. "Can you smell that, Clara? Doesn't fresh cut grass smell good?"

Lindsey looked beside her. The child was gone. "Clara!" She glanced over to the swing set. Empty.

Her eyes quickly scanned the chairs. The yard. The trees.

Nothing.

Her breath froze in her lungs . . . until a sound reached her ears.

Small fists pounded on the back door.

She swung around. Instant relief flooded her. "What are you doing, sweetheart? Do you want to go back inside?"

Round eyes full of fear moved up and down with her head. Lindsey opened the door and quickly shut it behind them. Her niece's fear was contagious. The hair on her arms now stood on end.

Lindsey followed her toward Elizabeth, but as she turned past a window she caught a glimpse of the far end of the yard. Her breath stalled. Were her eyes playing tricks on her?

She hurried to the door to lock it then peered out the window again.

Nothing.

Just an empty hammock, swinging in the still summer heat.

Books By Regina Tittel

Abandoned Hearts
The Ozark Durham Series vol. 1

Abandoned Hearts Study Guide

Unexpected Kiss
The Ozark Durham Series vol. 2

Love for Lenore
historical short story - ebook

Coming Sequels by Regina Tittel

Cherished Stranger
The Ozark Durham Series vol. 4

(Un-named)
The Ozark Durham Series vol. 5

Fear thou not; for I am with thee: be not
dismayed; for I am thy God: I will strengthen
thee; yea, I will help thee; yea, I will uphold thee
with the right hand of my righteousness.

—Isaiah 41:10

As always, thank you, Jerad.

Also, thank you to the continued support of our daughters and family, and to that special friend that inspired the purpose of this story.

And I would be amiss not to mention thanks to our Creator who gifts us with all good things.

Chapter One

A summer breeze caught Lindsey Buchannan's long, chestnut hair and flipped it behind her back as she stepped from the van. The afternoon sun flickered off golden highlights lending her an ethereal grace.

Keaton Durham stared through the window of the gas station and swallowed against the sudden dryness in his throat.

Someone gave a low whistle. "She's a looker, ain't she? You sure cain't tell she's had four kids. Not at all like my Betty." Snickers sounded from the other old-timers seated around the table.

One of the farmers beside Keaton poked his arm. "That's what you need, young man. A wife and a couple of kids."

Keaton twirled the remaining coffee around in his cup. He sighed and positioned his cap back on his head. "See you guys at the sale tomorrow."

He had to get out of here before she came in, or he'd give himself away. Lindsey Buchannan was the exact reason he didn't have a family. Why he was drawn to her, he didn't know. But it certainly wasn't fair.

Keaton's timing was off. He met her at the door.

1

Lindsey paused. "Why is it that every time we run into each other, you're always leaving?"

Keaton clamped his jaw shut. He was an honorable man, which meant he couldn't answer. With effort, he tore his gaze away before his eyes dropped to her beautifully molded mouth.

Life sure wasn't fair.

He tipped his hat without a word and stepped outside. A ten-commandment sign at the gas station entry whipped in the wind. Its tenth line served as his reminder . . . thou shalt not covet.

Purposeful strides took him to his Bronco. Why did she have to keep showing up in the same place as him? He honestly didn't want to take her from Mike. He was a much better man than that. But if he stuck around, he'd find himself wishin'. Wishing for things he had no right to want.

He slammed the door shut and gunned his rig out of the lot. Once he safely distanced himself from the station, he allowed his thoughts to travel back to a memory he often frequented. He'd first met Lindsey during the town's annual May festival. She hadn't realized he was in line ahead of her and crowded her litter of children to the front of the ticket booth to satisfy their eager pleas. He later learned they hadn't all been hers, but one could never tell by the way she treated them.

The oldest boy was the one who had noticed they'd skipped ahead. Lindsey turned with apologies and Keaton's heart was gone. Chocolate-colored eyes, accented by milky smooth skin had pulled him in, but it was something more that stole his heart. Unfortunately, he was certain she hadn't felt the same. Then to later realize she was married—it didn't make sense. Why would his heart flip for a married woman? Why would God allow that?

Two years later . . .

After six months of driving back and forth to St. Louis, the strain of traffic had diminished to little more than an annoyance. Lindsey now considered herself a seasoned city driver.

Her blinker signaled for the off ramp as she searched for an opening between cars. A woman behind the wheel of a SUV, oblivious to the surrounding traffic, bent her head toward her lap. One hand held a compact, while the other applied color to her eyes. Lindsey glanced at her horn. If she pressed it, the driver might react too quickly and cause an accident. She gritted her teeth. How unfair it was that while some battled for their lives from disease, others risked their's over vain pursuits.

Ten minutes later, she entered the hospital through rotating doors. The smell of disinfectant greeted her like an old friend. Tootsie, a senior citizen volunteer, smiled warmly. "Hi, sweetie, your Mike's having a good day. He's had two visitors already."

"Really?" Curiosity gnawed at the back of her mind as she hurried to the elevator. She stepped forward as the doors opened then remembered the greeter. Looking back, she called out, "I'll see you later, Tootsie."

Mike had been here so often, visitors were something of the past. Last week, though, his cancer had taken a turn for the worse. Perhaps people would start coming by again. Paying their last respects. What a horrid thought.

With a light tap on the door, she entered his room. "Mike?"

He stirred and opened sleepy eyes. "Oh, good, you're here." A frail hand patted the side of his bed.

Lindsey bent over to kiss his cheek before taking a seat. "Are you having a better day?"

Eyes full of acceptance implored her to understand. "There aren't any *good days* left."

Lindsey's eyes pooled with tears. She knew this day was coming, but denial had proven much happier than reality. What would she and the children do? She'd given birth to their first son soon after her high school graduation. They both agreed she should be a stay-at-home mom. One baby turned into four, then her sister's kids made six.

Six mouths to feed.

Mike's scratchy voice intruded her thoughts. "Hey, stop worrying, I've got a plan."

A nervous laugh escaped Lindsey's throat. "Oh, no. When you say that it always leads to—"

"I know, I know, something you don't agree with. Listen, Linds-," he started to cough and couldn't seem to stop.

Lindsey pushed the button for a nurse and rolled Mike over to his side. His body was so weak the coughing fit would sap him of any strength he might have left. The nurse arrived and administered a breathing treatment. Pneumonia had settled in his chest months ago and he still battled its effects.

Lindsey sat beside the bed and rubbed her husband's arm until at last, the nurse could leave. Mike's eyes grew heavy with sleep. How much longer did they have? Although she'd been filling the role of single parent for much of the last year, she still didn't feel prepared. Her gaze settled on the locked file box between the bed and the window. She didn't even know what was inside, only that Mike had instructed her to bring it the last time he was admitted. She rested her head against the cool bed rail and closed her eyes, letting her mind drift to the past.

They'd dated throughout her senior year. Mike was older and showed a true interest in her. His family didn't drink, they didn't smoke, and they definitely didn't take drugs. The exact opposite of her home-life.

Mike stirred beside her. "Good, you're still here."

Lindsey moved to sit on his mattress and ran a hand down his stubbled jaw. She blinked back the urge to cry.

"I want you to come back tomorrow with the kids." His voice was whispery and hoarse.

Tears began to fall. One by one, they slipped from Lindsey's cheeks and fell to the sheet below. Mike blinked several times. "Don't do this, Lindsey. Be strong. I need you to be strong."

She sniffed and nodded her head, unable to meet his eyes.

He tried to clear his throat but couldn't quite succeed. His voice came out thick. "You won't like what I've done, but I did it to take care of you and the kids."

Lindsey brought her head up. What was he talking about?

"Go home, now. I need to rest. Come back tomorrow with the kids." His voice faded as heavy lids closed over his eyes.

Lindsey released a heavy sigh.

"Mike," she whispered, "what have you done to me, now?"

***

Keaton returned to the city the following day. Was he making the right decision? Lindsey wouldn't take it well, and he couldn't blame her. But Mike was trying to do what he could while he still had the chance.

Keaton thought back to the day he described her to a couple of guys at work. "Do you know who she is?"

His two coworkers had exchanged glances. "Yeah," one of them said. "We know her. She's a real beauty isn't she?"

Keaton had stared past them, seeing a mental vision he often frequented. "But it's more than that. I think I could love a woman like her." He refocused. "Is she married?"

The men's eyebrows rose as humor danced in their eyes.

Then a voice sounded from behind. "Yeah, to me."

Keaton had spun around to face his boss, Mike, who stood a few inches taller. His build was lean in comparison to Keaton's solid frame. Still, he made use of his height as he glowered over him.

Keaton hung his head and rubbed the back of his neck. He looked up again with the side of his mouth pulled in a grin. "Well, Boss, you're one lucky guy."

"Uh, huh. Just keep your charm to yourself."

Irritation had prickled his skin. There was that word again. Charm.

For as long as he could remember, everyone had always called him a charmer. He took after his grandpa with eyebrows that slanted upward and a constant smile on his face. But his idea of a charmer was someone who manipulated people with their looks to get what they wanted. Something he would never do.

He despised the comparison.

The traffic light signaled green giving him an escape from the direction of his thoughts. He turned toward the hospital, arriving on time. He didn't know what to expect only that Mike had insisted he come back. Maybe he had more to discuss. His weakened condition only allowed for limited visits.

Inside, the elevator doors opened to the third floor. Keaton stepped into the hall and rounded the corner when Lindsey bumped into him. Tears streamed down her red face. He reached out to balance her but she jerked back.

"It's you."

He didn't know what to say. Obviously, Mike had told her his crazy idea. Keaton wanted to assure her he had nothing to do with it, but she wasn't about to give him the chance. "Lindsey, I—"

"Don't bother. I can't, I can't . . ." She brushed past him, probably unaware of where she was going.

A voice sounded from further down the hall. A boy, about seven, stood outside Mike's room. "Are you Keaton?"

He nodded, not trusting his own voice. Lindsey had been in tears, her heart was breaking, and although he wasn't the cause, he felt as guilty.

The boy stepped into the hall and met him halfway. "Dad's gonna die, and he wants you to be our new dad."

Keaton stalled. Yes, Mike had told him of his plan, but reality had yet to sink in.

Until now.

The boy straightened his back and looked him directly in the eye. "My name's Jack." His handshake was as firm as a man's, yet, he was just a boy.

Keaton pulled off his cap and ran a hand through his hair. His dark curls were beginning to tickle his ears. He needed a haircut. He slapped the hat across his knee then wound it between his hands. "How do you feel about this arrangement?"

The boy's swallow was visible. "I know we'll need a dad. And Mom will need help. Can you do it? There's a bunch of us kids."

Keaton rubbed the back of his neck. Could he? He'd dated off and on since meeting Lindsey, but never seriously. No one pulled a halt to his thoughts like she did. But was he dad potential, especially for six children?

He sighed before answering. "I guess that's up to your mama, son. I've prayed about it, and I didn't get a red light."

The boy's shoulders sagged with what appeared to be relief. Why was this so important to him? Shouldn't he have a problem with someone replacing his dad? Shouldn't he feel resentment and anger at the very idea? Instead, he seemed almost eager as he took Keaton's hand and pulled him toward the room. "Come on. Dad wants to talk to you."

Inside, the smell of old flowers permeated the room. The ends of their petals, now crinkled with wilt, stood as a predecessor of what was to come. Children were gathered around the bed. Some sat together in a chair, others beside Mike. The oldest girl held a toddler. The room fell silent. All eyes were upon him. He swallowed hard. Would he measure up?

Mike waved him over with a thin hand and tried to clear his throat. "I want you kids to meet your new dad."

Keaton couldn't help the tears that filled his eyes. This trustful man was handing his family over to him. He couldn't imagine the pain it must cause. Mike went through the names of each child, but Keaton couldn't concentrate enough to remember them.

"Mike, this . . ." He pushed his lungs against the heaviness that had settled on his chest. "This doesn't feel right."

Mike fastened pleading, sunken eyes on him. Skin that had lost its pallor now sagged against hollow cheekbones. He wouldn't make it through the week. "You promised." He started to cough. "You, you promised."

"I know, I know. But Lindsey . . . ," he swallowed against an upsurge of emotion, "she was so upset in the hall."

Mike stared out the window. "She'll come around. She'll have to. I made sure of that." His eyes slowly closed and his breathing became labored.

Keaton looked around at the expectant faces and forced his voice to cooperate. "Let's go. Your dad needs his sleep."

"Where are we going?"

Keaton looked down at the little girl who'd taken his hand. They were so trusting. So accepting. He wished their mom would be. "I bet you kids could use something to eat."

"Ice cream?" Questioning voices chimed in unison.

"Ice cream sounds great." Keaton led the troupe to the cafeteria. After a few confusing moments of ordering for six children, they were all seated at a table with ice cream for everyone. It amazed him how well-behaved they were. They didn't fight and helped look after one another. He supposed an illness would draw any family closer.

They'd just finished when Lindsey stepped inside the room. "There you are." She came to stand behind the eldest girl. "I went back to Dad's room and all of you were gone."

Jack stood to collect their trash. "It's okay, Mom. Dad fell asleep, so Keaton bought us ice cream."

She glanced in Keaton's direction but wouldn't meet his eyes. "You didn't have to do that."

"I wanted to."

The children picked up on the adult tension. Wide eyes and little ears took in everything. Keaton stood and emptied change from his pocket onto the table. "Hey, why don't you kids throw some pennies in the fountain while I talk to your mom?"

The children reached toward the coins. Lindsey kissed the top of her daughter's head and followed Keaton with slow movements to the row of windows on the other side of the room. She kept her arms hugged around her body and stopped a few feet away. As natural as he knew it was for her to want to keep her distance, it still stung.

He took a deep breath. "Are you cold?"

"No." She pressed her forehead to the window before the sobs took control.

Keaton positioned himself so the children wouldn't see her cry. Her obvious pain clenched his heart. Though it was difficult, he refrained from touching her. "I'm sorry, Lindsey. I know this is hard. I don't understand why Mike chose to do things this way."

A few moments passed, she sniffed several times and wiped her eyes. "I could do this on my own. I don't have to remarry." Lindsey straightened. "I'm in control of my own life. This isn't the turn of the century. People don't do this anymore!"

Her ranting wouldn't have made sense to just anyone, but Keaton knew exactly what she meant. Lindsey had allowed Mike to carry everything they owned in his name. Thus, giving him full control to do what he wished.

"You don't have to marry me if you don't want. You can find a way to work around this. He gave you a couple months. Talk to a lawyer. See what your options are."

"Don't you mean *we* could talk to a lawyer to find a way out of this?"

"No." He looked her straight in the eye. "If you want out, you're on your own."

Lindsey's mouth dropped open. "What are you talking about? Look at what you're getting." She gestured toward the fountain.

Keaton's gaze encircled the children and settled back on Lindsey. "I see a family. And the only woman I've ever wanted."

Chapter Two

The clock struck one o'clock reminding Lindsey she should be in bed. Two days had passed since Mike revealed his plan for her future, and she still couldn't wrap her head around it. She wanted to hope he wasn't serious, that he'd take it back, but she knew him all too well. Mike didn't think she was smart enough to do anything on her own, much less manage without a man to take care of her. But to expect her to move into another marriage so quickly? Honestly, what was he thinking?

Did his parents know what he'd done? They'd been there two weeks ago. Had he even hinted then what he expected her to do? Although her in-laws lived overseas and didn't keep in close contact, she still respected their opinion. She was sure they'd be disgusted, irate even, if she remarried within two months of their son's death.

I'm still up. I might as well call.

Her mother-in-law, Donna, answered on the second ring. "Lindsey, has something happened?"

"No. Oh, no, I didn't want you to think that." Guilt filled her heart. She hadn't even considered that they'd be expecting something worse.

"I'm sorry, Donna." She'd never felt encouraged to call her Mom, "I just wanted to talk to you."

"Okay. I hope it's not lengthy, as I have to take Bryan to his doctor appointment in twenty minutes."

Lindsey blinked back tears. She wouldn't feel sorry for herself. They didn't use drugs like her parents, nor had they ever encouraged their kids to. And Bryan, Mike's younger brother, had complications. He'd been handicapped since birth, so of course Donna's focus would be on him. At least that's what she tried to convince herself.

She cleared her throat. "Then I'll get right to the point. Did Mike mention anything to you about his plan if he doesn't make it?"

"Is my son near the end?"

"Donna, he hasn't come home since you were here over two weeks ago. He's pretty bad."

"Yes, I know. I was just hoping for a change." She sighed audibly.

"Have you talked to him recently?"

"I called on Wednesday."

Lindsey's breath stalled. She fingered with the worn, knotted fabric of her shirt. "Wednesday? Did he mention his plan for us?"

She could hear Donna shuffle the phone to her other ear and say something to Bryan. "No, he didn't. He couldn't talk very long. I'm sorry, Lindsey, but I need to go so we won't be late. I'll talk to you later. Tell the children hi for me."

"Okay." Her voice sounded small as she hung up the phone. If his parents didn't know, then it would be left to her to tell them. What would they think?

Would they help her out of her situation? Were they financially able? She knew so little about them. Mike's father had been in the military when they'd met. After his overseas tour, he and his wife had decided to stay in Europe. Their youngest son, though now in his twenties, needed a lot of care and the hospital they frequented provided excellent services. She didn't blame them. Nor did she miss them.

She shuffled toward her bedroom, shoving toys out of the way with her foot, a reminder of her failure as a housewife. The house never looked clean, even when it was. But that came with children. The joy they brought to her life far outweighed the small sacrifice of an orderly home. She wished Mike shared her views.

What little sleep Lindsey could get passed quickly. She dressed for the day and stood in front of the mirror. Her jeans sagged past her hips, even a belt didn't help. The kids would wake soon which meant time didn't allow her to sort through her drawers. Not that she had anything clean. Laundry day had been skipped again to visit Mike. She grabbed a box from the back of the closet labeled *pre-children clothes*. If memory served her correctly, there was a pair of stretch-jeans near the top. They'd get her through. She grabbed the first pair, but they weren't the stretchable fabric she expected. She tried them anyway.

Much to her surprise, they slid on easily.

Lindsey stared at her reflection. Due to her husband's illness, stress had taken its toll. Even the extra weight she hadn't been able to lose after their fourth child was gone. A tear slid down her cheek.

She'd take it all back, every ounce. Her children needed their dad.

A cloak of apprehension draped around her. As she stared at her reflection, fear stared back. Maybe Mike was right. Maybe she couldn't do things on her own. She had no idea how she would earn enough money for her family to survive, and accepting help from the government was the last thing she wanted to do. Food stamps and subsidiaries had been the way of her childhood. She wanted better for her kids.

A timid knock sounded from the other side of the room. It had to be sweet Clara, the child who had yet to speak. This was her way of letting Lindsey know she was up and probably hungry. Lindsey glanced at the clock before she opened the bedroom door. Six-thirty a.m.

No time for myself today.

"Hi, sweetie." She knelt to hug her niece good morning then held out her hand. "You want to help make pancakes?"

Clara's quick nod told her she'd chosen the right thing to say. The child grasped her hand and followed her to the kitchen where she climbed on a stool to help.

Lindsey had gained guardianship of Clara after her sister's death. Since that time, Mike had been in and out of the hospital. Little Clara still hadn't experienced a normal family. She used to think that once Mike got well, Clara would start speaking. But not even that was an option now.

What about Keaton?

Lindsey faltered with the measuring cup and flour spilled onto the counter scattering a blanket of white dust. A gentle hand tapped her shoulder.

"I know, Clara, Aunt Lindsey made a mess. My mind was somewhere else."

She hadn't seen Keaton since their shared visit at the hospital on Wednesday. Since then, she'd done everything she could to keep her mind away from him. *Obviously, I'm failing at that, too.*

By seven o'clock, the rest of the children were up and seated at the table. It was the weekend, so no school, and still the children rose early. Weary from the weight of an uncertain future, Lindsey sank into a kitchen chair and forced a smile until she felt it touch inside. Whether she was tired or not, her children were blessings and she was thankful for each one. She bowed her head. "Let's say grace."

After their prayer, Elizabeth, her six year-old, spoke up. "Are we gonna see Daddy today?"

Lindsey swallowed her bite of pancake, savoring the sweet mixture of butter and syrup, before answering. She opened her mouth to respond but the shrill of the phone interrupted. *Who would call this early in the morning? Unless . . .*

Jack answered the phone and held it toward his mother. "It's for you, Mom. It's the hospital."

Lindsey placed her fork next to her plate and rose on numb legs. Her son's solemn eyes latched onto hers. They both knew. She spoke into the receiver and forced herself to hear what she couldn't bear. Her shoulders began to shake as a hand covered her mouth. Jack aged ten years as he drew to her side and helped support her as they cried.

***

Keaton wrestled with the decision he'd made on Wednesday. One night of prayer on the subject wasn't much time before giving an answer. Still, he'd awakened with peace that morning. If only Lindsey had shown more support in her husband's decision. But he didn't blame her. If she had, that wouldn't have said much about her devotion to Mike.

He'd keep his word. What Lindsey decided to do was up to her. She had two months before the house and trusts set aside for their livelihood would go to a designated charity. If she married Keaton, it became theirs.

He didn't envy Lindsey's position.

The conversation he'd shared with his parents Wednesday evening resurfaced in thought. His mother had asked for the third time, "Are you sure you're making the right decision?"

"I'm sure." He's run a hand through his hair. "Lindsey's the one having doubts."

Keaton's father had leaned closer. "Son, marriage is a life-long commitment. When it comes time, make sure she's doing this to stay."

"She can't divorce me, Dad, if that's what you mean. If she does, everything still goes to charity."

His mother had shaken her head. "Poor girl. The turmoil she must be going through."

Keaton cleared his mind and strolled into the kitchen for his wake-up cup of coffee. It was Saturday, but no sleeping in with Ranger. At least he hadn't gotten mixed up again. Twice, earlier in the week, the rooster had awakened in the middle of the night confused by the full moon, and claimed it was sunrise.

Keaton stared at the cup in his hand. On its side, etched in gold ink, was the company's name where he and Mike worked. Mike had given them out as Christmas gifts to the entire crew this past year. Though Keaton had a deep respect for his boss, he didn't always agree with the way he handled things. Mike liked being in control. As a micromanager, he fought for his way on everything, down to the smallest detail.

Was that the kind of man he was at home?

It made sense. Even though Mike and Lindsey had been married for eight years, he carried everything in his name. He'd even made her bring the bills to him while in the hospital. Was she allowed to make any decisions? Did she have a voice in their relationship? Keaton didn't think so. No wonder it was so easy for him to arrange her future. Everything was under his control.

Mike had given Keaton a list of chores that needed to be done at the house, some of them small and insignificant that he was sure Lindsey, or even the kids, could handle without help. It was as if Mike didn't trust Lindsey to do anything without being checked up on. He'd wanted Keaton to stop by that week as often as possible, but he just couldn't. He couldn't impose on a family that wasn't his. Until Mike's last breath, they still belonged to him.

The phone rang and pulled Keaton from his thoughts. He listened to the hospital personnel on the other end of the line and hoped Mike's family made it in time to say good-bye. He pocketed his keys and headed out the door.

How would Lindsey take his presence? Mike had made it clear the staff should contact Keaton directly after her. Did she hate him? Or did she perhaps hold no opinion of him? He hoped for the latter. It would give him more to work with.

He'd wanted to ask why Mike had chosen him. But in his heart, he already knew. Two months previous, Mike had again been off work because of sickness, and had called in a favor.

"Hey, think you could drop by and cut up a tree in my yard? It fell over last week in the storm."

"Sure thing. Just tell me where you live." Keaton had thrown his saw in the back of the Bronco and gone to work. After he finished loading the cut wood onto his trailer, he visited with Mike on the front porch. Lindsey stepped out once to hand him a glass of tea. He tried not to stare as she'd turned to go back inside.

Mike propped his cheek in one hand and looked at Keaton. "Still think you could love her?"

Keaton was surprised Mike remembered his comment from two years earlier. He turned the glass around in his hand, swirling the liquid. "I'll get my own wife."

"But . . . you haven't."

Keaton had ground his teeth and stared across the yard in silence.

Mike shifted in his chair. "Stay single a while longer and you might get your chance."

"Don't talk like that." Keaton had risen from his seat. "I'll be seeing you at work."

He now sighed with the memory. Mike must have started his plan then, possibly even before. Had he actually called Keaton out to the house that day to reassure himself it would work?

The hospital came into view. Keaton parked his Bronco in the farthest parking lot available. He needed the walk to calm his nerves. Halfway across, he realized he hadn't considered the temperature. The July heat had already warmed up the pavement and it wasn't even ten o'clock. A light sweat began to prickle his skin before he made it to the doors. Missouri weather could never be depended upon, except for in July.

Inside the elevator, a shapely woman near his age tried to make conversation. "It's gonna be a hot one today." She fanned her blouse, stimulating her overly scented rose perfume.

Keaton saw her out of the corner of his eye but refused to give her attention. He simply nodded. He never could understand what women saw in him. Though he was broad and stout, he couldn't claim the height of his dad or brother. Nor did he take after them in looks.

The sugary voice tried again. "A dip in the creek would sure be nice."

The elevator dinged. He was saved. Keaton stepped forward as the doors opened. "Enjoy your swim." He imagined her disappointed look with disgust. Some people never think past themselves. *You're in a hospital, lady. People are sick. People are dying . . .*

He found three of the children in the waiting room. Red, swollen eyes confirmed what the staff had told him on the phone. The little girl who had taken his hand the other day rushed toward him and wrapped her arms around his waist.

Keaton froze.

Her sniffles brought tears to his eyes. He bent down and lifted her into his arms then made his way to a vacant chair. Her tiny limbs clasped around his neck as her tears dampened his skin. A young boy left the lap of his older sister and crawled onto Keaton's knee.

He was at a loss for words. Why were the children so comfortable with him?

As if reading his thoughts, the oldest girls said, "Dad's talked about you a lot." The older girl looked at the floor as she spoke. "He said you would teach Jack how to mow the yard. And sometimes we might even be able to see your cows."

Keaton swallowed against the lump in his throat. "What's your name, hon'?"

"Elizabeth." Bright green eyes met his. "I'm six. Josh and Samantha are four."

He looked at each child in his arms. "Are you two twins?"

"No." Elizabeth answered for them. "Samantha was Aunt Lauren's."

Keaton didn't understand, but the time for answers would come later.

Nurses milled about in attendance. Then Lindsey stepped through the door. She had a tiny girl on her hip and a son on each side.

"He's gone." Her voice was a mere whisper.

Josh slid from Keaton's lap and rushed to his mother. Keaton stood with Samantha. "I'm really sorry, Lindsey. Mike was a good man."

Blank eyes stared past him. She looked as though she couldn't take another step. Keaton reached for her elbow. "Come on, I'll drive you home."

He led them to the parking lot, all the while keeping a hand on Lindsey. He wasn't sure if it were more for her sake or his. But seeing her numb with pain tore at his heart. She must have really loved him.

The thought hit him like a blow to the heart. If she loved Mike this much, how would she ever be able to remarry in two months? How could he expect her to?

A heavy disappointment enveloped his soul.

Chapter Three

Lindsey brushed through her hair as she stared at the children playing in the yard. *To be a child again.* The whimsical thought played through her mind. Of course, through the freedom of her imagination, her own childhood would have a different setting than the one afforded her by reality. She, too, could run and laugh after healthy siblings. She'd be able to toss back her head while swinging without a worry for what her mother was doing inside. Or to what detrimental ends she was leading her other daughter.

She turned from the window and took in the haphazard state of her home. It was a wreck, and her in-laws were scheduled to arrive later in the afternoon. At least they'd made arrangements for Bryan's care. Even if she managed to get the house clean, the children's toys would pose a constant threat underfoot. Bryan would never have been able to manage.

Lindsey read through her daily list of chores that Mike had printed off then started a load of laundry. The sound of water rushing through the pipes nearly drowned out the ringing of the phone. The answering machine clicked on by the time she reached it. She fumbled with the off button in the middle of Mike's recorded voice. "Hello."

A moment of silence followed before someone breathed into the phone. "Sis. I hear you're about to inherit some money."

Lindsey gasped as a cold shiver ran up her spine. Clayton Turnbaugh, her sister's ex-boyfriend. He'd always given her the creeps and he always played that to his advantage. "Mike just died, Clayton. Whatever it is you want, can wait. We haven't even had his funeral."

He laughed in her ear, a sound devoid of any joy or happiness. "You still scared of me, little thing? That's good to know. Good to know. I'll be in touch." His whispery voice faded out before the dial tone sounded. Lindsey looked down at her arms and noted the hair standing on end.

Mike, you've always handled, Clayton. What am I going to do about him now?

A knock came from the front door, startling a cry from Lindsey.

The unlocked door opened as Keaton stuck his head through, his face etched in concern. "Lindsey, are you okay?"

She rested a hand over her mouth and turned away to catch her breath. "Yeah, you just startled me, is all."

"Can I come in?"

Lindsey turned around and dropped the phone into its cradle. "Okay, but don't trip. I've not paid much attention to the house lately."

Why did her stomach always flip when Keaton came into view? Right or wrong, even before Mike had become sick, the few times she'd seen Keaton her reaction was always the same. And though he possessed the incredible looks of someone you'd see on screen, it was more than that. Perhaps it was his genuine goodness that overflowed from the inside out.

Keaton stepped inside. He bent to retrieve a toy truck from the floor. "This looks like one I had as a kid." He fumbled it in his hands then looked up before continuing. "I stopped by to help out."

"Thanks, but I don't need any help." She glanced around the room and cringed. "Well, I guess that's calling the kettle copper."

Keaton smiled. "Mike mentioned you had your own set of clichés."

"What do you mean?"

She could tell he was trying to keep from laughing. He scuffed the heel of his boot against the rug by the door as he looked down again. "The way I've always heard it said is, that's the pot calling the kettle black." He brought his head up exposing his engaging smile. "Show me where the toys go and I'll get this room."

Lindsey stared at him in disbelief. "You're going to clean?" The thought was ludicrous. Men didn't clean. That was a woman's job. How many times had Mike drilled that into her head? She easily accepted it as truth. No one but her and her sister cleaned the house when they were growing up.

"Why not?" Keaton shrugged his shoulder.

She fought the small grin teasing the corner of her mouth. His eyebrows shot upward in an innocent look.

But was he innocent, or did he have another motive behind his offering? He'd said he didn't want out. Was he trying to soften her to Mike's crazy idea? "Why would you want to do that?"

He set the truck down and ran a hand through his hair. He needed a trim but somehow the tousled look seemed to add appeal. She shook herself and tried not to stare.

"I figured you'd be getting a lot of folks stopping by and . . . can't I help?"

Lindsey shook her head. She didn't understand him, but she wouldn't look a gift horse in the eye. Or was it the mouth?

"That basket in the corner is where most of this goes." She turned to point toward the loft. "And what doesn't fit can go in the toy box upstairs."

Her voice softened as she searched for the confidence to speak her mind. "And please don't think this will win you any brownie points. I can't marry you."

Keaton gave a polite nod and went to work. She stood with her fingers tangled together before she realized he wasn't going to rebuff her statement.

Strengthened by her small show of independence, Lindsey returned to the laundry. A few minutes later, Keaton had finished and asked for more instructions. She looked over his shoulder to appraise his work. The room was spotless. Even the children's drinking glasses had been removed and the end tables wiped down.

"Thank you . . ." His name was on the tip of her tongue but she couldn't bring herself to say it.

Jack stepped through the back door. "Mom, I saw Keaton's truck outside—"

"Keaton!" Samantha pushed past her cousin and ran toward her new hero. Lindsey watched with fascination as Keaton squatted down to receive her with open arms. Her niece clung to his neck with obvious adoration. The house filled with the rest of the children, all excited with his presence. Their voices rose in unison as each fought for his attention.

Since when had they become so attention starved? She felt a pang of something she couldn't put her finger on. The kids had never reacted to Mike's return in this way; no matter how long he'd been away.

Keaton cleared his throat. "Let's go back outside and play before we mess up the clean rooms."

He smiled at her as he walked past. It wasn't a smile of politeness, it went all the way through. He was as happy to see the children as they were to see him. A confusing emotion rippled through her heart. *What is it about him?*

Lindsey managed to change another load of laundry and dump the clean clothes on her bed before a knock sounded from the front door—again. Her breath stalled. With Keaton's appearance all thoughts of Clayton had vanished. Now the fear returned. Should she mention it to him? Shaking her head at the thought, she peered out her bedroom window.

Her shoulders sagged with relief. It was members of her church with pans of food. She opened the door wide to invite them in. Laverne and Lilly exchanged greetings with her as they entered the front room. At that moment, she was very thankful for Keaton. His efforts had saved her from embarrassment.

"We brought some casseroles, dear. Now these can be easily frozen. And you might want to do that. Luella and Olga Jean will be stopping by as well, but I'm not sure what they made."

Lindsey's eyes pooled with grateful tears as she accepted a dish. She was so thankful for their little country church. She swallowed, unable to speak. Lilly pulled her into a tight embrace and pounded her back. Lindsey fought to balance the casserole to the side.

"Honey, we knew it was a comin', but we're so sorry. Now you let us know if there's anything we can do, ya hear?"

"Yes, I will." Once released, Lindsey swiped her tears with the back of her hand.

She saw the women glance about her house. Laverne waved her hand toward the open rooms. "It looks like you've kept things up pretty well. But is there anything we can do, such as floors or look after children. Where are those children anyway?"

Lindsey stalled. She hadn't given any thought how to explain Keaton to her church family. "Actually, one of Mike's friends stopped by and is playing with them out back while I ready the house. Mike's parents are coming in this afternoon."

The women nodded in understanding and took their leave. Lindsey gathered the casseroles and strode to the kitchen. Would they have accepted the news as easily if they'd seen Keaton? Probably, not. He possessed the looks of a heart breaker.

Did that thought come from me?

Familiar tears gathered in her eyes. She despised the predicament her husband had created. How was she supposed to mourn Mike if he already expected her to move on? How much easier it would have been if he'd lived.

Easy? Really?!

A small voice niggled her conscience. She tried to squelch it, but it begged to be heard. Life hadn't been easy with Mike. She often dreaded the time when all the children would be grown. The kids were the only thing they'd shared in common.

She swept the thought from her mind. There would be plenty of time for that later. Right now the house demanded her attention. She searched for space in her freezer then groaned at the disastrous kitchen. Laundry could wait, but the smell in here had to go.

***

The viewing lasted for hours. Lindsey's feet throbbed from standing so long. People from work continued to file in and offer condolences. Never had she hugged so many strangers before. They might not have been strangers if Mike had allowed her to attend the work parties with him. She swallowed back bitter memories.

She glanced over to where part of her children sat with his parents. Elizabeth was such a blessing. She sat beside her grandmother with Clara on her lap. Originally, Donna had tried to befriend Clara but was met by tears. That act wouldn't win Clara any favors. Lindsey knew her mother-in-law well enough. Her whole demeanor could turn if things didn't go her way.

Lindsey's eyes trailed the room in search of Keaton. Wherever he was, she could be sure her other children were with him. She glanced once more. His absence brought a small, unexpected disappointment.

She refocused on the conversation of the man in front of her. He was reminiscing about a trip he and Mike had taken. If only he knew how much she'd always resented Mike's trips. Instead of family vacations, he'd gone hunting with "the boys."

The ache in her legs climbed to her hips. She winced and shifted her weight. Before she knew it, Keaton was by her side. "Looks like you could use a break. How about you tend to Bradley? He doubts my skills. I'm sure Mike's parents can take it from here."

He smiled politely at the man before guiding her to the side, not waiting for her to protest. She glanced back at her in-laws. They were already in her place.

"I spoke with them first." Keaton's words fanned the hair that hung over her ear.

All she could do was nod. He led her to the restrooms. "Bradley's in the men's room, but I'll stand guard out here."

Lindsey stepped through the door with caution, hoping it was empty of any unsuspecting males. "Bradley?"

"I'm in here, Mama."

She found her three-year-old in the far stall. After helping him get clean they returned to the hallway where Keaton kept three men waiting in line.

Lindsey felt the heat of embarrassment rise to her cheeks. "Sorry about that."

She turned her gaze to Keaton. "And thank you . . . Keaton."

He gave her a gentleman's nod then turned his attention to Bradley. "I think your mom could use something to drink. You want to show her the snack room?"

"Yeah, come on, Mama. They got tinkies'!"

Keaton showed his winning smile. "I learned there's more than one name for Twinkies." He held open the door. Inside, the rest of her children were seated in the floral upholstered chairs watching a cartoon on a portable DVD player.

"Wow, someone was thoughtful. I wonder who brought this in." She smiled at her contented kiddos.

Keaton turned toward the sink to fill a glass with water while Jack answered. "Keaton brought it."

Lindsey stared at him in awe. He cleared his throat. "I know these things can be kinda long for kids. So I borrowed it from a friend." He bent his head and rubbed the back of his neck. "I hope you don't mind."

"It . . . it's fine." Never had she been around someone so thoughtful and considerate. Something about it made her uncomfortable. She downed the offered water and made an excuse to leave.

Another hour passed before the funeral home closed its doors. Phase one of the mourning process had been initiated. If only her tears hadn't been so selfish. She hadn't cried for a lost love, as she was sure everyone assumed. Her tears had been for the confusion of her current state. It didn't seem fair. She had abided by God's law. She'd stayed true to her marriage vows, tried to be a good wife and mother—despite life's challenges and Mike's constant disapproval. Why did this have to happen?

She didn't have an education. Aside from the small jobs she'd held in high school, she didn't even have work experience. What would she and the children do? She'd have to talk to Mike's parents. Surely Donna and Michael would help her find a way out.

Lindsey and her in-laws drove home in relative silence. Their eyes had belied their curiosity when she'd allowed Keaton to drive her van home an hour earlier with the children. But now wasn't the time for explanations. Her father-in-law was seated beside her while Donna stretched out as much as she could on the back seat of the Bronco. She knew they were tired. Jet lag, topped with the funeral of their son, had to be emotionally, as well as physically exhausting. Their conversation would have to wait.

A light from the television flickered in the front room of the house. Lindsey stepped through the door and stopped. Keaton was seated in the middle of the couch with his legs stretched out in front. Her children were in various positions on each side of him, and the other furniture. But what made her heart pause was the one sleeping on his chest.

"Clara?" Donna's voice sounded next to her ear.

Keaton's eyes fluttered open. Lindsey hadn't realized he'd been asleep, too. He put his finger to his lips to signal for them to be quiet. Donna pushed past Lindsey with disgust and went down the hall toward her room.

Keaton stood, careful to keep from jostling Clara awake. He approached Michael and whispered, "Could you help me get the rest of these rug-rats to bed? Then I'll be on my way."

Michael nodded in silent agreement and carefully picked up a sleeping Bradley. Lindsey led them up the stairs and pulled down the children's bedding. Tonight had taken its toll on everyone.

When at last the children were tucked in, Lindsey walked Keaton to the door. "Thank you for all your help. I have to say, I was amazed to find Clara asleep on your chest. What charms did you work to win her over?"

The tired but friendly smile fell from his face. "I don't use charm."

Lindsey stared up at him, surprised. His serious, almost sad expression probed her curiosity. "Sorry, I wasn't trying to offend you."

"I know." He lifted a corner of his mouth and gave the nod of his head that was becoming more familiar to her. "Good night."

***

Keaton arrived home, his stomach in knots. He opened the refrigerator door, stared at the nearly empty contents, and grabbed the last can of soda. Just as well, since lack of food wasn't the problem. Standing so close to Lindsey as she thanked him was. It took all of his control not to touch her. Now he was free to love her, but he still had to hold back. Give her time to mourn.

From stories the children had told him, he was beginning to understand part of their family's history. Lindsey's sister had died leaving two daughters in her care. They looked enough like the other children it was hard to believe they weren't all siblings. Though, the youngest one's quiet ways were haunting. No child that young should be so withdrawn. What cruel lessons had life taught her?

Keaton flinched from the cold liquid on his hand. He'd unknowingly crushed the can he held and spilled its contents. The children had already made themselves at home in his heart. He hated to think of anyone ever causing them pain. One thing was for sure, under his care, they would always be protected.

The next few days went by in a blur. Work was chaotic. Everyone had pulled together to make things work while their manager, Mike, was sick. But now that he was gone, the workers fought over his position like grade-schoolers.

Keaton turned away and shook his head. If they only knew. The position had already been offered. The decision sat between Keaton and Dale. Upper management watched their progress and the decision would be made in a few, short weeks. To secure Mike's job would be a huge victory for Keaton. His goal of becoming a manger would be met and his time and effort devoted to the company would finally pay off.

His cell phone vibrated in his shirt pocket. Out of habit, he answered without glancing at the number. "Hello, Keaton here."

"Keaton."

The small voice pricked his heart. "Elizabeth?"

"Yeah. Daddy gave Jack and me your number in case we ever needed you."

Keaton moved toward the exit. The factory's interior noise made it too difficult to hear her soft voice. "What's wrong, sweetie?"

"Mama fell asleep with Clara. And me and Jack saw a man look in the window."

Alarm tensed his muscles. "What man, hon? What window?" He took off toward his truck.

Her voice was just above a whisper. "The scary man."

Chapter Four

"I'll be right there. Tell Jack to make sure the doors are locked and don't open them to anyone but me."

Keaton waited until Elizabeth hung up before ringing George, their stand-in manager from another department. Before now, no one had asked questions concerning his connection to Mike's family. Now the rumors were sure to fly with people wondering why Mike's kids would call him.

Lindsey only lived fifteen minutes from town, but Keaton still kept the pedal pressed to the floor, slowing only when needed. Had Mike's parents already left? Two days had passed since they laid Mike to rest. Surely they planned to stay longer.

He turned down the country road and arrived in the Buchannan's driveway in record time. Lindsey's van was the only vehicle in sight. Keaton turned off the truck and scanned the perimeter. Who was the scary man? More importantly, *where* was he?

He gave a soft rap. The door was a nine-light, so the children would easily see him though the panes of glass. One by one, the tops of their heads peeked out from beneath the kitchen table. The front area of the house was one large room separated as a living room and dining room, all visible from the front door.

Keaton waited for Jack to unlock and swing it open. "Where's your mom?"

"She's still asleep. We tried to wake her but she wouldn't wake up." Fear flickered in his eyes.

Keaton's breath stalled as his world came to a halt. "Where is she?"

Jack pointed to the door partially closed to the left of the living room. A few quick strides and he pushed it further open. The bed sat against the opposite wall. Lindsey rested on top of the covers with Clara snuggled up to her side. Keaton stood in the doorway and watched their breathing. Assured they were actually sleeping, he allowed himself to take a full breath.

How had it come to this so quickly? She was his future. He couldn't bear any harm to come to her.

Keaton turned to Jack and counted the rest of the children to make sure they were all there. "Tell me what you saw."

"We've seen him before. He doesn't come around very often but when he did, Dad always ran him off. He's real scary looking."

"Where was he?"

Jack pointed to the window overlooking the back yard.

"Stay in this room. I'm going to have a look around. Under no circumstances do you come outside. Got it?"

After Jack agreed, Keaton crept out the back door. He knew whoever had scared the children was already gone. Everything felt too peaceful.

Still, he strode to the end of the yard and walked a couple of feet into the woods. Positioned so the house was still in view, he stopped beside a tree and listened. Determined all was well, he turned to leave.

A ground bird fluttered upward not two feet away. Keaton glanced at it and spotted the white flesh of a broken branch. He stepped around the few trees that blocked his way. A slightly worn path trailed from further into the woods to the yard. Whoever it was, this hadn't been their first visit.

Keaton made a mental note to return and check it out after Lindsey woke up. But for now, he'd let her get a much needed rest. Only after he rejoined the children and knew they were still safe did he allow himself to relax.

Samantha tugged on his hand. "I'm hungry. I want a apple."

He smiled at the sight of her little hand in his. "Let's go see if we can find one."

The children led him to the kitchen. Dishes dirtied the sink and remains of lunch littered the cabinet. Elizabeth brushed past him and opened the refrigerator. She distributed apples to everyone.

Samantha tugged on his hand again. "I want mine cut up."

"All right." Keaton withdrew a knife from the holder on the counter. He sliced it into pieces then began removing the core.

"What are you doing?" Elizabeth pushed back long hair so much like her mother's and furrowed her brow.

"Taking out the seeds."

"Why?"

Keaton jerked his head to the side. "So you don't have to eat them."

"We always eat the seeds. Mom says they're good for us. They taste good, too."

"Yeah," piped in Samantha, "like cherries!"

"If you say so." He placed the cut apple slices in a bowl and handed them down. "Now I'll see if I can get this kitchen clean for your mama."

Jack left the small table where the children were seated and stood beside Keaton. "Thanks for coming over. I feel a lot safer when you're here."

Keaton stopped loading the dishwasher. "Where's your grandparents?"

"They needed to take a drive by themselves. They said they'd be back by dinner."

Josh, the boy a year older than Bradley pushed out his bottom lip. "I wanted to go, too, but they wouldn't let me."

Elizabeth settled the matter. "That's because they need time to be sad."

"I'm not sad." Samantha smacked her bite of apple. "I like our new daddy!"

Keaton bent to look under the cabinet for soap. He wasn't sure how to take her compliment. Their dad had been sick for so long, it probably made her feel secure to have him around. Still, Mike hadn't been laid to rest long enough to encourage her opinion.

He grabbed the dish detergent, filled the washer and turned the dial to start.

The children asked for a movie and he was glad to oblige. He was still shocked into silence by the child's statement. Why hadn't the others argued with her? Stepping back inside the kitchen his thoughts were stalled by the dishwasher. Like a deep sea monster from some low grade film, bubbles foamed over the top in waves.

"Oh. Uh . . . oh no!" He ran over and used his hands as buckets, shoveling suds into the sink. But no matter how fast he worked, soap bubbles continued to roll out the top.

Jack appeared by his side and began shoveling as well. He called to Elizabeth, "Hey, Sis, we could use some help in here!"

"Sshhh, you'll wake up your mama." Keaton smiled down at his helper whose eyes were lit with excitement. It was contagious. Keaton felt the laughter build until he was laughing so hard it was all he could do to keep shoveling.

"What in the world—" Lindsey stopped in the doorway with Clara on her hip. Josh scooted past her and slid on his knees in the pile of foam.

Keaton straightened and moved to stand in front of the washer. "We . . . ere, I . . . uh." He glanced down at the suds rising around his boots. With a half grin, he raised his shoulders and palms.

Lindsey stepped further inside the kitchen as Keaton's feet slipped out from beneath him. She reached for his hand but lost her footing as well. Clara landed on top of his chest and they lost themselves in a fit of laughter and bubbles.

Keaton held on to Clara and pulled himself up then reached a hand for Lindsey. Bubbles clung to them everywhere.

Clara's giggles made the sweetest sound. The child was lit up like a Christmas tree.

Keaton glanced at Lindsey and saw tears in her eyes. How long had she been waiting to hear her niece's voice?

Lindsey asked through hiccups of laughter, "Let me guess, you used liquid, dish soap?"

Keaton hung his head in mock shame. Before he could answer, a sound from the other side of the room captured their attention.

"Ah-chem."

Keaton looked up as the surrounding laughter died away.

Donna and Michael stood in the kitchen entrance, their countenance void of humor, and sucked all joy from the moment.

***

Lindsey's smile fell from her face. Their scornful glare was something she'd experienced all too often. She tried to turn off the dishwasher with fumbling fingers. They shook too hard to be of any help. Why did she always feel like a failure in the presence of her in-laws?

Keaton's hand covered hers as he flipped the aged handle of the dishwasher to its off position. His contact gave her a quiet strength she wished she could hold onto.

He cleared his throat. "I was trying to be helpful. But obviously, I don't use a dishwasher at home, and well . . . wrong soap." He glanced at the solemn faces of the children. "How about you guys get dry clothes on, and I'll meet you in the backyard."

"Can we play in the sprinkler, Mama?" Elizabeth's eyes looked hopeful, as if wanting to hang on to the fleeting moment of happiness. "The boys are already wet."

Lindsey easily capitulated. Anything to get them outside and away from the demeaning lecture she was sure to receive.

Donna and Michael seated themselves at the dining room table, not bothering to hide their impatience while the children and Keaton went outside. Never once, did they offer to help with the kitchen mess or with the children's swimwear. Lindsey sighed and stood behind a chair with her hands braced on the back for support. It was her fault for taking a nap.

"Sit down, Lindsey." It wasn't a request, more like a military command. Michael pointed to the seat of her chair.

She preferred to remain standing but lacked the confidence to defy him. Like the rest of her furniture, the chair had seen better days and creaked in response, even to her light weight.

Donna spoke first. "I don't know what to make of you. You've changed so much from the daughter-in-law we used to know. I guess an illness can do that, but I hope this change isn't permanent."

Lindsey felt the throb of a headache begin above her right eye. "What are you talking about, Donna?"

"Your mother-in-law," Michael overstated, "is referring to homeschooling for starters. We realize Mike wasn't in his best frame of mind this past year. And I do realize that pulling them out of school gave him more time with the children, but now that he's gone, I assume you'll return them to school this fall."

Lindsey swallowed and wished for a glass of water. "Actually, no. We fell behind because of Mike's condition and still need to finish up. I don't know exactly where we'll be by the beginning of the school year, and I don't want to risk Jack and Elizabeth being held back."

Donna's eyes widened. "If you don't want them held back, then do the sensible thing and put them back in school. Lindsey, you're not cut out to homeschool. Really, who is? It's a distorted view of education, if you ask me."

"Well, I didn't ask you." Her voice was small but firm. Surprise at her ability to stand up for her children quickly turned into fear. How would her in-laws respond?

Donna's mouth fell open then she turned to her husband for support. Before he could say anything, Lindsey tried to better explain. "I enjoy having them here with me. I also like the fact that I'm in control of what's going into their minds. Last year I had to deal with so many issues that shouldn't have needed addressed until junior high at the earliest."

Michael slapped his hand on top the table and jumped to his feet. Lindsey's shoulders scrunched toward her ears. "Lindsey, you don't have Mike anymore. You need to stop acting so ignorant about your situation. You're going to have to get a job. You can't very well do that with children at home. And it would help to get rid of the extras. You've done your good-will service. Now it's time to let the state handle them."

As though a bucket of cold water had been thrown at her, Lindsey began to tremble. But this time, it wasn't from fear. Anger, unlike anything she'd ever known, colored her cheeks and threatened to spill forth from her mouth. She took a controlling breath against the wave of heat that consumed her, and through up a quick prayer for patience. "I'll have you know, I don't have any, *extras*, as you called them. Samantha and Clara are *children*! *My* children."

The tremors of emotion couldn't be calmed, tears brimmed her eyes. How dare they do this to her now? She'd just buried her husband. Clayton was already haunting her. And she still felt groggy from the pill Donna insisted she take. She stood to leave but Donna's acidic words halted her exit.

"And I suppose you've already replaced our son."

Lindsey's stomach sickened as she yearned to crawl into a hole. Hide away from these nasty people and their stilted views. *God, help me.* In a small voice she spoke over her shoulder, "I need to talk to you about that."

She returned to her seat and waited until her father-in-law did the same. Her throat ached for the tears she held inside and her stomach rolled with anxiety. "Mike did something without my agreement, and I need your help to get out of it." She took a deep breath and explained the situation Mike had legally created.

The color drained from her in-laws' faces. Michael swallowed visibly, but his disbelief quickly turned into anger. He slammed his fist onto the table with force. "How could you allow this to happen?"

His next words were ground out. "How could you be so naïve? He certainly couldn't have been in sound mind. You should've protected him from this."

Lindsey's mouth hung upon for a brief moment. This was unbelievable. "Protected him? More like, myself."

Lindsey rubbed her forehead against the increasing headache. Her voice openly shook. "Listen, I had no control over it. He made it legally binding and only told me about it a day or two before he died. But, now I need your help. I don't have the money to fight this. We, I mean, I, still have part of his hospital bills to pay. I can't afford a lawyer."

Donna shook her head. "I think it's outrageous you'd ask us. Between the flights here and Bryan's care, we aren't in any position to help."

Michael stood and encouraged Donna to her feet. "Get rid of the extras, agree to put the children back in school, then talk to us."

Lindsey's voice continued to tremble as tears tracked her cheeks. "You know I can't do either of those things. You're asking too much."

"And I think you like your fate. We've noticed more than once the way you and that man look at each other. And before I'm tempted to assume more has already gone on, I think it's time we draw our stay to a close. We've already scheduled our flight for tomorrow. We'll say good bye to our four grandchildren and find a motel for the night."

Lindsey stood too numb to move. Her vision registered them walking away while everything else became a blur.

Her fate was sealed.

Chapter Five

Keaton stood poised by the door with Clara's blanket scrunched in his hand. He hadn't meant to eavesdrop when he'd slipped inside. Michael and Donna's footsteps registered them coming closer. He remained where he was. If they accused him of listening in, he didn't care. He had something to say, and he would say it.

Michael drew to a quick halt, surprised to see Keaton, and cleared his throat. "We have nothing to say to you. We're telling our grandchildren good-bye."

"You'll tell all of them bye, or none at all." He thrust the blanket toward him. "And since this is what I came in for, now you can take it to Clara."

The two men stood across from each other, Michael unwilling to suffer his pride and Keaton determined to uphold the girls.

Donna moved past her husband. "Come on, Michael, they're just children. We'll say our good-byes then we'll leave."

Half an hour later, the Buchannans were gone. Lindsey prepared spaghetti while Keaton stayed outside watching the kids. He still needed to explain why he was over, but they hadn't had a chance to talk.

She stepped through the back door to call everyone in for dinner. Her face looked drawn and sad. He despised her in-laws for the stress they'd heaped on her frail shoulders.

Frail?

He took a closer look at the woman he'd willingly give his heart if she'd only accept. She stood with her spine straight and took charge of her six children. She'd had a very rough year, but had seen it through.

No, she wasn't frail at all. Lindsey Buchannan was strong and beautiful. *Oh, so beautiful.*

Buchannan. He didn't want the name attached to hers any more. Lindsey Durham sounded much better. The thought brought a smile to his lips.

The evening passed quickly and Keaton helped the children to bed. He shuffled his feet, by the front door. "Would you step outside with me? I need to talk to you."

She nodded and dropped her gaze but not before he saw the sheen of tears. She was overburdened with stress, and he was about to heap on more. How would she take the news about the prowler? He stepped outside and glanced around the remote setting. How could he keep them safe?

Keaton motioned to the glider under a nearby tree. "Let's sit down."

Lindsey's feet didn't move. She stared at the two person swing in disapproval. He almost laughed. She showed all the trepidation of an ending to a first date. "I don't bite, Lindsey, and I promise I won't try to kiss you."

She turned toward him. Through the light from the porch, Keaton saw a mix of emotions cross her face before she finally gave him a small smile and walked with him to the glider.

He gently rocked the swing as he decided where to start. "I'm sorry for what your in-laws put you through today."

"You heard?"

He clenched his jaw. The anger they'd instilled still hadn't left. "They had no right to speak to you like that, or about the girls."

Lindsey wiped her cheeks as silent tears spilled forth. "They never supported that decision. But Mike wanted Samantha and Clara as much as I did."

"What happened that made you their mother?"

Lindsey wrapped her arms tighter around her body and shivered despite the hot July evening. "My parents were into drugs. My whole life that's all they knew. And though I resisted using them," she paused and closed her eyes for a long moment, "my sister didn't."

Keaton drew in a deep breath. He couldn't imagine the little children nestled inside going through something like that. And to know Lindsey had, tore at his heart. "Where is she now?"

"She died a few months ago. Like our mother did two years earlier, Lauren overdosed." She sniffed and clasped her hands together on her lap. "And in case you're curious, my father is alive and well . . . in prison."

Lindsey turned toward Keaton, meeting his gaze through the shadows. "If you're smart, you'll leave now before the children snag your heart. You owe us nothing, you've been kind to help, but don't chain yourself to us because of something Mike talked you into."

Keaton stopped the rhythm of the swing. "I was already snagged. But the children aren't to blame. You are."

Her mouth formed an o shape matching her wide round eyes. Keaton stood from the swing and took a few steps to distance himself. She was too appealing and didn't even know it. Of course the children had snagged his heart, too, but it was Lindsey he'd always loved. He knew if he stayed seated beside her, he wouldn't keep his word. Her lips were far too tempting.

He rubbed the back of his neck. "I'm glad Michael and Donna are gone, but you've got another problem."

"Aside from losing my house and money?"

Keaton glanced back. "You're not going to lose anything."

Their eyes met in a silent battle. Keaton was determined to marry her. Lindsey was determined to stand on her own.

"There's more at stake than that, Lindsey." He returned to his seat. "The reason I'm even here now. The kids called me today because someone was prowling around outside."

She gasped and glanced around the darkened yard. "Where is he? When did this happen?"

Keaton took hold of her hands and claimed her rapt attention. "You were still asleep and Jack and Elizabeth saw someone look through the window from the back."

He felt her hands tremble. Had she expected this? "You said, *he*. You know who he is, don't you?"

"What am I going to do, Keaton? Mike always took care of this." Her weak voice shook with fright.

"Took care of what?"

"Clayton Turnbaugh, my sister's ex-boyfriend . . . and Samantha's biological father."

***

Keaton had returned inside with Lindsey to double check all the window and doors locks. Her safety system was lousy. The doors featured a lock on the knobs and nothing more.

Speaking to the interim manager again, Keaton asked for another half-day and Friday off from work. He had enough time on the books he could take off a month if he needed to.

He pulled into Lindsey's driveway and saw small heads bobbing up and down in the window. The children had been thrilled when he'd called and asked to stop by. Though Lindsey was more hesitant, he could still detect relief in her voice. This Clayton person had her scared.

The door opened and the children ran outside in one loud chorus shouting his name. Keaton laughed at his newfound fan club. He had never realized how dull life had been until now.

He reached the steps and met Lindsey on the porch. She was dressed in cotton shorts and a t-shirt, and still looked beautiful. "Am I interrupting their school?"

She flipped a glossy lock of auburn hair behind her shoulder. "We just took a break."

He tried to read what thoughts swirled behind her chocolate gaze but was too distracted by the children. Josh jumped on his back and tried to help pull Bradley up with him.

Keaton looked over his shoulder. "If you monkeys climb down, I'll let you help me install these dead-bolts."

"Whoo-hoo!" The boys' feet were on the ground in seconds.

Lindsey narrowed her eyes. "Locks? I don't recall asking you to do this."

A smile tugged at Keaton's lips. "You didn't. Consider it a gift." He raised his hand against her objection. "You need them. It'll keep you all safer and ease my mind."

Her eyes stayed narrowed as if judging his reasoning. "But shouldn't you be at work?"

Keaton gave instructions to get the boys started then turned back to Lindsey. "I took the afternoon and tomorrow off."

A softness blanketed her face. "For . . . for us?" She gestured to the children.

"Yeah. Why's that so hard to believe?" Her reaction was a mixture of amazement and admiration. Those were good emotions to build on, but all because of a couple days? Had Mike ever taken time for his family?

Samantha tugged his hand. "Can I help, too?"

"Sure. Let the boys help with this door, and girls get to help with the back door."

He glanced back at Lindsey. A sweet look of awe still graced her face. There was so much to learn about each other. Why did the small acts he performed mean so much to her? What kind of life had Mike given her, and how could he make it better?

Keaton's arms ached to hold her. To let her know how much she meant to him. How valuable she was. But he couldn't. Not yet.

***

Lindsey peered out the kitchen window. True to his word, Keaton had taken Friday off, not for himself, but to spend with them. Now he tugged on the cord of the weed eater until it revved to life. She turned to the window on the other side of the room to check on Jack. Keaton had put him on the riding lawn mower and she'd been furious.

She had run outside with no other thought than to save her son from getting hurt. Keaton had grabbed her arm and pulled her to a stop. "It's okay. I taught him what to do."

She stared at him in disbelief. "You're the one who put him on that thing?"

"Yeah. Why not?"

"Why not? Because he's never ridden the lawn mower before! Mike wouldn't let anyone near it. He'll hurt himself."

Keaton placed his hands on her shoulders and turned her to face him. "I'm out here with him. He's only allowed to mow the flat surfaces in first gear. I won't let him get hurt." He paused. "But if you really don't want your son mowing, we'll get him off."

Lindsey stared after her son rather than be drawn into Keaton's caring gaze. He was nothing like Mike. He allowed her to make the call. More than that, he entrusted her son with a worthy responsibility. No wonder the children accepted him. He made them feel important. He made them feel loved.

Assured Jack was okay, she left the window to check on the other children and run from the unfolding thought. *He makes you feel important. He makes you feel . . .*

She wouldn't allow herself to go there. Love was a false emotion. Her parents hadn't shown it, Mike had never said it.

Her conscience struggled against the truth. There was love between her and the children. There was love between her heavenly Father and herself. Love wasn't false. It just wasn't always fair.

The back door opened and Keaton stepped through. Sweat dampened his shirt and trickled from his brow. The smell of freshly mowed grass mingled with the spicy scent of his aftershave. "Lindsey, we ran out of gas. If you don't mind, I'll take Jack with me to get some more."

"Me want to go." Samantha, his ever-present shadow, was determined to be included. The only reason she had been inside was because of the yard work being done. Keaton had told her he didn't want to chance a rock kicking up and hitting her.

Josh and Bradley chimed in behind her. "We want to ride in your truck!"

Keaton smiled and shrugged his shoulders toward Lindsey. "You might enjoy the break."

She admired the excited faces of her children and knew she couldn't turn them down. How long had it been since they'd had something to look forward to?

Elizabeth stopped by her side with Clara on her hip. "We'll stay with Mom, right Clara?"

The toddler looked between Lindsey and Keaton as if she couldn't decide. Say it, Lindsey silently willed. *Just one word. Tell us what you want.*

Clara remained silent, reached for Lindsey and grabbed a fist full of her hair for comfort. "Okay, guess that's all you have room for anyway. Don't forget to transfer their booster seats over."

Keaton gave her a nod of his head. "Got it. Be back in a jif."

Lindsey stood rooted to the same spot. How had they become so comfortable with each other in such a short amount of time? The children, of course, had a lot to do with it. The image of him leaning through the doorway with a hand on either side of the door-jam teased her senses. The sinewy strands of his muscled arms had bulged from the exertion of yard work. Whether he liked being described as charming or not, he definitely had that appeal. But equally as strong, was his honest nature. There was no guessing with Keaton. So different from Mike.

"Mom." Elizabeth's soft voice halted her thoughts from embarking on the negative aspects of her marriage.

"You want to know what's left to do in school?" Lindsey acknowledged her nod and instructed Elizabeth on what pages to finish. She glanced about the house to decide which chore to attack, but the strange quiet left by the rambunctious young-ones' absence made her uncomfortable.

"Honey, I'm going outside with Clara to replace the yard furniture where Jack finished mowing. We'll be right back."

She stepped outside and settled Clara on the lawn next to her and moved the chairs back into place. The toddler kept pace with her back and forth to the house for the first couple of chairs. "Can you smell that, Clara? Doesn't fresh cut grass smell good?"

Lindsey looked beside her. The child was gone. "Clara!" She glanced over to the swing set. Empty.

Her eyes quickly scanned the chairs. The yard. The trees.

Nothing.

Her breath froze in her lungs . . . until a sound reached her ears.

Small fists pounded on the back door.

She swung around. Instant relief flooded her. "What are you doing, sweetheart? Do you want to go back inside?"

Round eyes full of fear moved up and down with her head. Lindsey opened the door and quickly shut it behind them. Her niece's fear was contagious—the hair on her arms now stood on end.

Lindsey followed her toward Elizabeth, but as she turned past a window she caught a glimpse of the far end of the yard. Her breath stalled. Were her eyes playing tricks on her?

She hurried to the door to lock it then peered out the window again.

Nothing.

Just an empty hammock, swinging in the still summer heat.

Chapter Six

Clayton's dark, vengeful face loomed everywhere. His mocking smile laughed at Lindsey's vulnerability. Had he actually been in the hammock? That would mean he'd been there while she and Clara were outside. And he'd cleverly waited until Keaton was gone.

The phone rang and Lindsey jumped. She had to get a handle on her nerves or she'd pass her fear onto the girls. After a deep breath, she reached for the receiver. "Hello."

"Your hammock's right comfy, sis."

"Clayton," her voice shook as the cold, clammy hand of fear took hold, "tell me what you want then leave me alone."

"Money. I'm itchin' for a fix, but I'm low on cash. And I believe you're in a way to help me."

Her eyes darted toward the window as she tried to swallow the desire to cry. "If you only knew the mess I'm in you would never ask."

"But I have asked, so now it's your problem to find me some money." His voice held a menacing threat. "You wouldn't want me making a stink about you raising my daughter, would ya?"

An unstoppable tremor snaked its way through Lindsey's body. "What are you talking about? I've been raising Samantha for most of her life."

"But I'm her real daddy. If you don't help me out, I'll make trouble for your little home-sweet-home." A sick chuckle followed. "And if my guess is right, that second one belongs to me, too."

Lindsey slammed the phone down and took a step back. "No," she whispered, "Lauren, you promised you were done with him."

She stared at the phone, afraid it would ring again. Bile rose in her throat. Was he still out there, or had he left to make the call? No, he wouldn't have had time. She ran upstairs and collected two baseball bats from the kids' room. She placed one by the front door and was intent on placing the other one near the back when Clara appeared with a thumb in her mouth and her blankie held tight in her sweet little fist. "It's time for your nap, isn't it?"

Lindsey dropped the bat, picked her up and crossed to the rocker. She was glad for the distraction. Was he still out there? Common sense told her he'd call again. She fought off a shudder and snuggled Clara closer. The child's eyes grew heavy with sleep after the first song.

Lindsey smiled down at the little cherub. She'd never let any harm come to her. Dark blonde lashes spread across pale cheeks like feathers against a cloud. Clouds that never released a drop of rain. Life had taught her that crying wouldn't make any difference. No matter how many tears she'd shed, her mother wouldn't answer them. Lauren's life of drugs had kept her in a different realm than that of her children.

Lindsey had often prayed her sister would turn to Christ for strength and overcome her addictions, but it wasn't to be. Only three months earlier, her body had finally given out, tired of the years of poisonous abuse.

Lindsey thought back to Clara's birth. She had been there for the delivery wanting to support Lauren. Lauren's oldest child, Samantha, had already been in Lindsey's care under a legal guardianship for two years Somehow Lindsey assumed Lauren would relinquish care of the baby to her as well. But when Clara arrived, Lauren wouldn't give her up.

She remembered Lauren telling her, "You can't take her, Linds'. I know I'm not a good mother, but if you take her, I won't have any reason to get clean." Her meth addiction had left holes in her teeth and her clothes hung off bony shoulders. She was a mess and Lindsey had forced herself to hold back tears as she'd looked at her.

She recalled staring down at the new-born sleeping in her arms. So peaceful. So innocent. So undeserving of the life she was born into. "You have to get help, Sis. For Clara's sake, get help."

A strong resolve filled her as she stood to lay Clara down. She couldn't lose her nieces. She'd do whatever it took to keep them safe. Safe, and away from Clayton Turnbaugh.

Even if it meant giving him money.

Keaton returned with the children each carrying a bag of groceries. Lindsey crossed the room to open the door and raised an eyebrow at him. "What are you up to now?"

He flashed his heart-melting smile. Did he know how irresistible that look was? She doubted it.

He put his hand on her son's shoulder. "I thought after Jack and I finished with the mowing, we could all run to the river for a swim and top it off with a wiener roast."

Elizabeth left the table where she'd been busy coloring. "Yeah! That's a great idea. Hurry up and finish mowing."

Lindsey smiled at her daughter, glad to have something nice to think about. She put a hand on Keaton's arm but withdrew it with a sudden sharpness. *Had he felt that?* Her hand still tingled. "Keep him close to the house."

"Do you need to tell me about something?"

She looked up and saw him glance at his arm and shake his head.

"I mean, did somebody stop by?".

She knew what he was getting at as his head jerked toward the baseball bat lying on the floor near the door. She also knew he'd felt the electric connection between them, but didn't seem surprised.

Lindsey hadn't prepared herself for his questions. Did she want his help? It would only involve him on a deeper level with her family. She didn't need to entangle him more if she wasn't going to marry him. Her mind made up, she took a bag of groceries to the kitchen and called out over her shoulder, "No, I've got everything under control."

"Jack, we'll mow in a minute. Right now I've got to check something out." Keaton passed Lindsey and headed for the back door. He paused before stepping over the bat lying in the floor. He gave her a knowing look before picking it up and opened the door to the backyard. "Lock this behind me."

She stopped and dropped the grocery bag to the floor. How did he read her so easily?

Lindsey turned the dead-bolt behind Keaton and watched him jog across her yard to the woods. *Lord, keep him safe.*

"Mom, where's Dad going?"

Lindsey turned to stare at Josh. "Wh–what did you call him?"

Her four year old looked up with innocent eyes. "Dad."

Jack walked up beside him. "He's going to be our dad, right? That's what our first dad said."

Lindsey rubbed her forehead, not sure of what she should tell them. "I don't know about that. This is all too soon. I'd appreciate it if you would just call him, *Keaton.* Right now you need to remember your real dad as much as you can."

Jack frowned. "He never let me mow."

"Yes, well, he did other things with you."

The argument died on Jack's lips before he even started when thunder sounded. All of them turned to the window. The sky had darkened and the trees shook in the wind. *Keaton, please hurry.*

Lindsey refocused Jack on finishing his school work while the other children put away the groceries amidst complaining about the weather. The brewing storm meant their fun at the river would have to wait.

Twenty minutes passed, and still Keaton hadn't returned. Would Clayton hurt him? Even if he wanted to, Lindsey was sure he'd be no match for

Keaton's strength. Keaton was built like a solid wall. His broad shoulders looked as though they could carry the weight of the world. And his well-defined arms . . . *Whoa, what am I doing? My husband's been gone for little over a week and my mind's already thinking like this?*

Lindsey strode to the kitchen to decide on dinner. She had to do something to keep herself busy. There was still a casserole in the freezer left from someone at church. That would have to do. She pulled it out as Jack rushed to her side.

"Mom, Keaton's running through the rain."

The dish teetered in her hands, but she managed to keep from dropping it and set it down. She raced to the back door and held it open as he stepped through. He was drenched.

"I didn't expect the rain."

The children clamored around him. "Can we get wet, too?"

"No." Lindsey turned them toward the other room. "I need you to play while I talk to Keaton."

Josh turned back. "You mean, *Dad.*"

Lindsey felt the heat build in her neck, knowing Keaton heard. "No, we talked about that. Now go get *Keaton* one of your *dad's* t-shirts."

She turned back around and caught Keaton's expression. It was a mixture of honor and humility. Under different circumstances, it would be too easy to fall for this man. She steeled her heart once more and cleared her throat. "So, what did you find?"

Before he answered, Josh returned with a white t-shirt. Keaton reached for it. "Thanks, buddy."

He pulled his wet shirt over his head then twisted around to hang it on the doorknob.

Muscles rippled across his tanned back. Lindsey tried not to stare at his well-toned body but found it impossible. He was beautiful.

Keaton pulled the dry shirt on and fingered his hair giving his curls a semblance of order. Lindsey was still staring when he crooked a smile at her. "Thanks."

"Wh–what for?"

He shrugged. "For the unspoken compliment."

Lindsey rarely turned red, but if the heat in her cheeks were any indication, she was now crimson. "Well, Mike had such a lean frame, the shirts never–they didn't . . . you fill them out really nice."

She dropped her gaze to the floor. *Uggg. Way to go, Linds.*

"Thank you, Lindsey."

His soft, sincere response made her look up. Their eyes locked. His were so full of love. His openness made Lindsey want to cry. Here was a man who was everything she could hope for, all the things she never dared dream about, but she wouldn't allow herself to want him. She couldn't.

Pride told her she had to make it on her own while guilt reminded her she'd be a pitiful person to even consider Mike's plan.

She turned to look out the window, intent on diverting Keaton's attention. "Where did the path go?"

Keaton sighed then moved to stand beside her. He was so close their arms nearly brushed against one another. "It led to the county road. There're tracks where a truck had pulled off to the side. And the path is more worn. He's been here before and more than once.

Lindsey let her head drop to the cool window pane. How long would the money she planned to give hold him off? She only had a small amount of cash left.

"What's this guy after, anyway?"

"I'll take care of it."

"Lindsey," Keaton again spoke with a gentle voice, "I know you don't like the idea, but I would be able to keep you safe. If you'd only—"

Lindsey shook her head. "It's nothing personal, Keaton, because you're a wonderful person, and you've already proven you'd be a great dad to the kids. But I'm not ready. This is all too soon."

Would it be wrong to admit she'd felt so completely controlled by Mike that now she wanted to experience freedom? Before she could decide, the words fell from her lips. "I've felt suffocated for so long under Mike's finger—What? I can tell you're trying not to smile."

"Sorry, I think you meant to say, Mike's thumb."

Lindsey felt her mouth draw upwards. It was hard not to smile around Keaton. The man always looked happy and had a way of drawing smiles out of everyone, even Clara.

"How do you plan on keeping the house?"

Lindsey's gaze switched to the wall, seeing nothing. "I don't know. I don't even like this house, but it's a roof over our heads. I thought I'd talk to the bank this week, see what my options are."

"Do you have someone to watch the kids?"

"No, but I'm sure I can take them with me."

Keaton lifted his hand and fingered a lock of her hair. Lindsey closed her eyes. It'd been so long since anyone made her feel special—*had she ever felt truly special*—she wanted the moment to last.

"Don't try so hard to be independent or you'll lose out on making someone's day by needing them. Someone like me." He took a step back. "I think I'll head home."

Without thinking what she was doing, Lindsey stepped toward him. "Why? You could stay for dinner."

Keaton's gaze dropped from her eyes to her mouth. "Cause if I stay, I'll want to do this." He bent his head and touched his lips to hers. His mouth was gentle and enticed her to respond. They soon parted then met again. Keaton broke the connection and moved back.

Lindsey blinked several times to try to clear away the confusion left by his affection. "You're not making this any easier for me, are you?"

Keaton smiled and gave a nod of his head. "That's the plan."

"But Keaton, I won't . . . I can't marry you."

"We'll see."

***

Lindsey arrived home from church, the following afternoon, exhausted. Thanks to Keaton's kiss she hadn't slept well the night before. The touch of his lips sent shivers straight through to her heart. His lips had been tender and hesitant with the first kiss. The second kiss had held a glimpse of what the future could hold.

"Mom, why are you rubbing your mouth?" Elizabeth looked up, her eyes centered on her mother's hand.

Lindsey paused, unaware of what she'd been doing. "Oh, I was thinking, sweetie. And I guess it's time I stop thinking and find out what papers are in your dad's box."

Her bare feet scuffed against the chipped linoleum flooring to the kitchen table. Apprehension slowed her movements. She stared at the box before unlocking the lid and flipped it open. Sitting on top of the rows of files was an envelope with Mike's hand writing, addressed to her. Could it be a love letter? She hoped not. After treating her like a mere acquaintance at best, a bothersome duty at worst, it would be an insult. But that was her fault . . . at least, that's what Mike had always said. With hesitant fingers, she peeled it open.

Lindsey,

The bills have been paid forward for two months. I've also set it up with the bank to have your monthly allowance deposited into a new account under your name. With this account, you will have your own checks but I recommend that you stick to using cash.

I know you're probably thinking of how to get out of marrying Keaton, but this is for your own good. You don't have what it takes to do this on your own, you need him. Marry him and everything will work out fine.

Also, my truck has been paid for. You can ask Keaton to have the title switched to his name, as well as the house.

Take care of everyone,

Mike

Lindsey bit the inside of her lip to keep from crying. Feeling sorry for herself never improved anything, she didn't need to start now. But it would be so easy.

The thoughts pushed their way through her feeble defenses. What was wrong with her? Why wasn't she loveable? When in a moment of weakness she had asked Mike, his answer had been, *"If you could ever do anything right, I might learn to love you."*

She swiped at silent tears and whispered aloud, "I tried. I really tried."

Bradley crawled into her lap. "Who talkin' to?"

Lindsey sniffed and shoved the note to the side. "No one, Bradley. Not anymore."

Mike was gone. She didn't have to answer to him ever again. But he still held a strong hold on her. His written words were like a taunt in the back of her mind. "You don't have what it takes—" Was it true?

Jack yelled from the living room. "Mom, Keaton's here . . . and somebody's with him!"

With a tentative act of defiance, Lindsey removed her wedding band and tossed it in the box. She shut the lid and shoved it aside. Bradley slid from her lap and crossed the room with her. As she opened the door, her heart dropped to her feet. Standing beside Keaton was a beautiful, blond woman with large aqua eyes.

Had she lost him already? She closed her eyes for a brief moment. *You didn't want him anyway.*

Remember? Still, a wave of jealousy surged through her.

Chapter Seven

Lindsey glanced at her attire, thankful she was still dressed for church. The flirty gingham dress was a sale item left over from two years ago. It had taken several months of scrimping, but she'd been determined to make the purchase. The dress was one of the few new items she'd ever bought.

She cleared her throat and forced herself to say hello to Keaton and the woman by his side. But she couldn't paste on a smile. Even after all her years with Mike, she couldn't act like him and pretend everything was okay when it wasn't.

Keaton stood smiling, as though he were the proudest man alive. She should slam the door in his face, but something held her back.

"Lindsey, I'd like you to meet Lucy, my little sister."

A rush of air left Lindsey's lungs. "Oh. It–it's nice to meet you. Please, come in."

Lucy nearly danced across the threshold. "Keaton's told me all about you, I'm so glad he finally agreed to bring me out here." She squatted on her haunches to talk to Samantha before Keaton entered.

Lindsey looked from Lucy to Keaton. Why was he here with his sister? She raised a brow at him. "What's going on?"

He stopped inches in front of her and brushed a finger along her cheek. "Trying to make life easier for you. Lucy loves to help out." He took a step back and admired her dress. "You're beautiful, Lindsey."

Warmth spread along her limbs, tickling her skin. *He really means it.* Lindsey held his gaze, wanting to be drawn in more until one of the children's laughter drew their attention.

The children acted half shy and half like show-offs. They were also clearly enamored by Lucy's beauty. It seemed to shine from somewhere deep inside and radiate outward, drawing the children's trust like bees to pollen. No, bees to flowers . . .or maybe honey. Whatever . . .

Keaton's voice sounded close to her ear. "Lucy's great with kids and if you need her, she'll watch them while you talk to the bank this week."

Lindsey's jaw dropped. She turned to look up at Keaton. "Why would you do this? Why would you ask her . . . do you want out?" A sudden disappointment sapped her strength. She didn't want him to give up, but she wasn't about to venture why.

Keaton took a step closer. "I told you I don't want out. That's not going to change. But I figure the sooner you find out what you can or can't do, the sooner you can move on to a decision."

His gaze searched her eyes then dropped to her lips. Was he going to kiss her in front of the children and his sister? He sighed and took a step back. Lindsey shivered against the chill left by his distance. One day soon, she would have to deal with her thoughts and why it was that every time Keaton distanced himself an overwhelming sense of disappointment claimed her.

"Lindsey." This time it was Lucy's voice that interrupted her thoughts. "Let's leave Keaton with the kids so we widows can chat."

Lindsey allowed Lucy to take her by the arm and lead her away from the others. "You're a widow, too?"

"Yep, over a year now. Mine had a heart-attack. I heard your husband died of cancer."

They both took seats at the table. "Yes, he did."

"That gives us conversation for another day. But now, let's talk about something else. My brother said you were strong and brave and determined to survive on your own, but you need to talk to the bank first. So, that's where I come in . . ."

As Lucy continued to talk, Lindsey's mind replayed what Keaton had said to Lucy. He thought she was strong and brave? No one had ever called her either of those things before.

"Are you still there? You-hoo, Linds'?"

Lindsey smiled at the ball of energy beside her. Lucy was so confident with herself, even calling her a nick-name already. She could already see a great friendship forming between them.

"Are you okay? You look a little funny." Lucy eyed her with suspicion.

"No, I'm fine." Lindsey blinked against the onslaught of tears. "It's just been a really long time since I've had a friend. Mike wouldn't allow me to have, well . . . that doesn't matter anymore. I'm so glad to get to know you. Thank you for being here."

Lucy reached over and hugged her. "We may have more in common than I thought."

Lindsey sat back against her chair and looked at Lucy. An unspoken message passed between them that only they could understand. They'd both had to deal with controlling husbands. And now, they were both free.

Yes, this could be the beginning of a great friendship.

***

The week was nearly over when Lindsey finally had her appointment with the bank. It had taken two days for someone to return her call. She stood in front of her mirror and wiped sweaty palms over her slacks. Her gaze returned to the blue-jean cut-offs cast aside on the floor.

"You've got to be kidding me." Lucy shook her head. "Don't even consider those old things. This is business. You have to approach these people like you're as important as they are. And believe me, if you walk in there looking like Daisy Duke, they'll all be cursing you for your good looks, not helping you."

Lindsey smiled weakly. She hadn't eaten all day, her stomach was too wobbly. Could she do this? Mike had always told her he was the one with the business head. That it would all go right over hers. What if he was right? What if she wouldn't be able to understand anything? She'd look like a complete idiot.

Lucy appeared in the reflection of the mirror and placed a hand on her shoulder. "We went over everything. It's not complicated."

"If you say so."

"Is something else bothering you?"

"I don't feel like me." Her black slacks were topped with a white and black blouse. Lucy had pinned her hair up in a French knot and insisted Lindsey wear makeup.

"You've got class, Linds. Now, stop worrying and go strut your business self or you'll be late."

She laughed at Lucy, who was beginning to feel more like someone she'd always known rather than someone she'd met less than a week ago. "Lucy, I'm not a business woman."

"But you're going there for business, so get your business attitude in place. Don't forget to keep your shoulders high, you're going for intimidation."

"I can't be intimidating."

Lucy turned Lindsey's shoulders to face her. "But if you don't at least try, they'll walk all over you and you won't have a chance at changing anything."

A devilish smile stretched across Lucy's face. "Which would be to my benefit, since I'm rather fond of the idea of having you as my sister-in-law."

Lindsey waved off her comment. "You sure you won't come with me? You and the kids could wait in the lobby."

"Well, that would be intimidating, just in another way." Lucy pretended to talk to an imaginary bank teller. "If you don't give us what we want, we're going to let them loose."

"Okay, okay, I'm going."

"And take your time. If you need to stop anywhere afterwards, do it. We'll be fine."

The sound of a toilet lid slammed loudly from the other room, followed by mischievous laughter. Both women exchanged worried looks.

Lindsey rounded the corner with Lucy on her heels and saw two blue-headed children run from the bathroom. "Stop! What have you two done now?"

Samantha and Bradley, stopped inches from the back door. Samantha, the more versed of the two, turned an innocent look in her direction. "What wrong, Aunt Lindsey?"

"What's wrong? Both of you are wet and colored blue." She stared in disbelief. What could they have gotten into this time? Though she would never want to lose her niece, Samantha's presence added a whole new element to her family that not even all her boys put together could rival.

Lucy moved around her to open the back door and usher the guilty party outside. She sniffed the air. "That smells like—Do you have a blue cleaner in your toilet?"

A small moan escaped from her throat. "I just bought it the other day and I've regretted it ever since. Clara was starting to use the potty on her own but now is afraid of the blue water."

Lucy glanced in the bathroom. "While those two find it fascinating."

Lindsey peeked over Lucy's shoulder and moaned again. Blue water drenched the floor and walls. "I don't even want to know what they've been doing."

Lucy pushed her back out. "You've got to go. I'll take care of this."

"No way," Lindsey shook her head. "I can't leave you with this mess."

"What, you think I was agreeing to baby-sit six angels? I'm smart enough to know when you get this many kids together, there's going to be mishap and mayhem."

After useless objections, Lindsey said her good-byes and turned down the road. She was still awed by Lucy's goodness. She supposed it ran in their family, considering Keaton's good heart as well.

Minutes later, her nerves returned at the thought of her current errand. The silence inside the van became suffocating and did nothing to help. Although she had left the children in the church nursery a couple of times to visit Mike in the hospital, she'd never gotten used to the lack of noise. Not even the radio could penetrate the unusual stillness. The feeling left a gaping hole inside her, stealing her confidence. She wished Keaton was with her. His presence gave her a quiet strength like no other. A voice seemed to intrude in her conscience. *I can give you strength.*

"Oh, Jesus, I haven't leaned on you enough. I'm sorry about that." She continued her conversation in the confines of her mind while she drove.

Please help me through this. And if I can't find a way out, thank you for Keaton. He's a wonderful man . . . but I don't want to be in another relationship like I was with Mike. If I ever remarry, can't I have the fairy-tale? Is it too much to ask?

Everything's so confusing, Lord. I want to please You, but I don't know what the right thing to do is. Is it wrong to want to love someone so soon after Mike? Is it wrong to keep my kids from having a great dad? Is it wrong to wait and have more time to get to know Keaton?

"Uggg," she slapped the steering wheel, "life is so complicated!"

The bank came into view and brought with it a swirl of butterflies in the pit of Lindsey's abdomen. She checked her appearance in her rearview mirror, not recognizing the face that stared back.

In an effort to be taken seriously, and at Lucy's insistence, she'd applied a light layer of makeup, something she hadn't done in a very long time. Mike hadn't allowed it. The makeup made her eyes appear brighter and her skin looked healthier.

As she stepped into the bank, she held onto a mental picture of her reflection, and the confidence it brought. A fresh bouquet of mixed flowers greeted her at the door. Their pleasant perfume calmed her nerves and relaxed her tight muscles. She introduced herself to a lady at a desk and was soon seated behind a nameplate in scripted with, Sheila Grossman.

Ms. Grossman entered the room and eyed her up and down. Was she basing her opinion toward Lindsey on her appearance? *If so, thank you, Lucy.*

"Now what is it I can help you with, Mrs. Buchannan?"

"I'm in a peculiar predicament." Lindsey explained her situation and watched Ms. Grossman's eyes as they changed from disbelief, to sympathy, to all business. At least she had emotions. "I need to know what my options are. Can I take over the house payments? Do I have any rights to the account?"

"Let's see what we can do for you. May I call you Lindsey?"

"Of course."

"And you can call me, Sheila. We might as well get comfortable, as this may take a while."

Lindsey fidgeted in her chair while Sheila typed on her computer. The clicking of the keys continually intruded on her thoughts. Just as well, since she wouldn't know what steps to take until she had an answer to start from.

What if she did get to keep the house? How would she make the payments? She could sew. Homemade purses were selling really well, but a new business like that would never pull in enough to make the house payments. Perhaps she could start a daycare in her home. It wouldn't be very different from a normal day.

The computer keys finally came to a rest and Sheila swiveled her chair to face Lindsey, a disappointed smile on her face. "Nope. I'm really sorry, Lindsey. But no matter how I try to work the system, bottom line is you can't refinance something when your name isn't on the loan or deed. And even if I could somehow get my manager to agree to let you, you'd still need twenty percent of the loan as a down payment. Let me check one more thing."

Lindsey looked down at her hands in her lap and swallowed hard. She couldn't take over payments. She had to basically buy the loan from her deceased husband. But even if they allowed that, she'd need . . .

"Sixteen thousand dollars. That's how much you would need, and it's in your husband's account, but unless you meet his stipulation you won't be able to access it. And if you meet the stipulation, the house becomes yours anyway."

The facts swirled around in her mind as her mouth hung open. Mike had at least sixteen thousand dollars in the account? She glanced at the attire she'd borrowed from Lucy just to be taken seriously. Most of the clothes in her home had come from thrift stores, yet Mike had hidden this kind of money all along? Did the woman seated in front of her realize Lindsey didn't know this, and that it was probably wrong to even tell her? She clamped her mouth closed.

Her mind returned to the earlier information. There was no way out. Lindsey swallowed against the lump in her throat. Mike had thought of everything, and he would get his way. Keaton was getting what he wanted. The only one whose opinion still didn't matter was Lindsey's. Nothing was going to change.

She rose on numb legs and thanked the woman, whose name already slipped her mind, and stumbled out the door.

She stepped into the main lobby and waited her turn for a teller. Mike said her weekly allowance would be in an account set up for her. Hopefully she wouldn't appear as ignorant as she felt. Mike always handled the business end of everything.

Once the money was tucked inside her purse, Lindsey headed out the door, thankful the trial was over. She mentally calculated how much she could spare for Clayton. It wasn't impressive, but she had to restock their groceries and Mike never allotted her any extra. That had to be asked for, then explained in detail then waited until he decided if it was a worthy expense. Even death couldn't stop his control.

She sat in her van with the air conditioner running and ran the facts through her mind once more. Three weeks had already passed. That left a little over a month before she'd have to marry Keaton.

Keaton.

It was time to face reality. What was so wrong with marrying Keaton?

She didn't have a choice.

It was too quick.

Neither of her answers said anything negative against him. They were only matters of pride.

Okay, God, You got me on that one. So what's the positive about Keaton? A warm smile spread across her face as his image filled her mind. He's incredibly handsome. He helps me clean. He's funny and sweet. He encourages my opinion and listens to my voice. The children love him, he loves them . . . and he loves me.

He loves me.

Lindsey drove toward home hardly aware of her surroundings. Instead of going straight to the house, she detoured on the gravel road and slowed to a stop near a half mile from her house. Like Clayton had said, a rusty coffee can sat lopsided on the ground against a sycamore tree. Had it not been for its white and black trunk, she would've never known where to look.

She glanced in both directions. He didn't know what time she would be here, still, she felt someone watching from the shadows. The idle of the van's engine resounded in her ears. Could she do this? Better yet, should she do this? It was her only choice. Clayton had threatened to fight for custody. Logic told her the court would never grant it, but she'd heard enough horror stories to know custody cases didn't always end fairly.

The van door creaked as she pushed it open. Once she placed one foot on the ground, the rest of her actions sped by in less than a minute. She clamored back inside the safety of her van and pushed her lock button several times. The money was now sealed inside the can. Her hands trembled as she pulled the lever from park to drive. Curiosity begged her to look back. Her imagination taunted her with the sight of Clayton stepping out of the shadows, having been there the whole time. Lindsey shoved her hand against the rearview mirror, adjusting it upward and concentrated on the road. If he was there, he could keep himself company.

A sigh of relief escaped her as her home came into view. Though she'd never been in favor of its purchase, it now stood as her beacon of safety.

She pulled into the drive as Elizabeth rounded the corner of the back yard with Clara on her hip, waving hello. Lindsey paced herself to keep from running to them, but she couldn't control her hugs. She embraced them both and listened to her daughter chatter about all the fun they'd had with Lucy.

"I'm glad everyone had a good time." And that they were safe. Clara reached for Lindsey, for which she was thankful. She inhaled her sweet toddler scent and stepped through the front door followed by Elizabeth.

"Did you have fun, Mama?"

Lindsey furrowed her brow. "Fun?"

"Yeah, without all us kids."

She blinked back the sudden sensation to cry. "No, honey. I missed all of you. I always feel lost without my chatterbox gang." She returned her daughter's smile.

Satisfied, Elizabeth pinched her wet swimsuit away from her body and headed for the back door. "I'm drying out, and you know that's bad for dolphins."

"Right. I'll see you outside after I change." Clara wiggled in her arms. "Clara's coming with you."

Lindsey made a quick stop inside her bedroom and changed into her cut-offs and a loose, cotton shirt. Now she could relax. She settled in a lawn chair beside Lucy and accepted the proffered glass of lemonade.

Lucy checked out her change of clothes and smiled. "That was fast. So, I take it you're glad to be home."

She sighed as she watched the children run through the sprinkler, her mind adrift in thought. "Mike made sure I couldn't change anything. I guess he did it for my own good. He wanted to make sure we'd be okay."

Lucy snorted. "Hardly."

Lucy's bold sarcasm surprised her. "Why would you say that? Did you know him?"

Lucy shook her head. "You still haven't figured it out, huh? Your husband was an emotional abuser, Lindsey, like mine. He didn't set this plan up to protect you. He did it to control you."

"I know the way Mike treated me wouldn't have won him any awards," she furrowed her brow, "but I wouldn't say he was abusive. Lots of people are treated so much worse. He never even hit me."

"Girl, the sooner you own up to the facts, the better off you'll be."

Jack ran past them in a spray of water. Both women laughed and wiped water droplets from their arms. Lindsey was glad for the interruption. She wasn't ready to admit that she knew Lucy was right. They spent the next few minutes talking about the children, a safe topic. But her thoughts soon drifted from the kids to Keaton.

"Lucy, how can all the right things be here and I still want to fight against them? What's wrong with me?"

Lucy raised a brow. "Is this connected to the bank?"

"Oh. No. Now I'm thinking about Keaton." She filled her in about her experience with the bank and her thoughts of Lucy's brother.

"You've read too many fairy tales."

"You're right, I have. But that's what I want. I want to be the princess."

Lucy giggled. "I think we'd have to rewrite your fairytale. You'd need more than a horse to ride off into the sunset with your prince and six kids." They laughed together at the mental picture. "And your prince would have to have really broad shoulders to bear that size family."

Lindsey nodded her head in agreement, still humored by the thought.

"He'd need a big heart to take everyone on."

Her nod came slower.

"Of course, he'd be handsome, have a great smile." Lucy grinned and gave a sidelong glance. "And if he already had a home on a farm it would help with giving the story a classic appeal. A nice white house could represent a castle rather well. Don't ya think?"

"My house is white." Keaton appeared from around the front of the house and stopped where they were seated. "What are you girls talking about?"

He leaned down and kissed the top of his sister's head, though his eyes never trailed from Lindsey's. She half hoped he would treat her to the same. Though he'd called during the week, it'd been five days since she'd last seen him. His hay fields had kept him busy. Until now, she hadn't realized how much she'd come to depend on him. He brought an unexpected happiness to her home; a completeness.

"Hi, Lindsey." He smiled his charming grin before squatting beside his sister.

Lucy bounced up from her seat and turned toward the house. "I'm thirsty, be back in a bit."

Keaton chuckled and took the vacated seat. "Sis. She's not very subtle."

Lindsey tried to pull her gaze away, but couldn't. The sight of him made her heart beat faster and gave her such peace at the same time. She longed to touch him, to feel the familiar spark that ignited between them each time they made contact, but pride kept her fingers laced together in her lap.

Keaton cleared his throat. "Did you go to the bank today?"

"Yes." She looked away and pretended to absorb herself in the children's play.

"What did they say?"

"Hmm . . . I believe, nope, was the word." From the corner of her eye, she noticed a smile pull on the side of Keaton's mouth.

"What?"

Lindsey glanced over at him, shocked by the blatant hope written on his face. She turned away again, his goodness was too surreal. "I can't take over payments of the house. And there's no way I can gain access to Mike's account. He's covered all the bases."

Keaton released a loud sigh. "That's great news for me, but how do I convince you?"

Chapter Eight

Keaton wanted an answer from Lindsey but knew not to expect one. Still, how would he convince her they could make things work?

He slid his hand beneath hers and watched her gasp from the contact. She felt it, too. The connection they shared was unlike anything he'd ever experienced. Had she felt this with Mike? Hopefully not, since he wanted this to be as new for her as it was for him.

Her round chocolate gaze widened as she stared at him. Could her silent questions be the same he'd asked himself?

"You can always trust me to be faithful, to listen when you speak, to lo—"

A thick spray of water soaked the front of Keaton's shirt, followed by war cries. Before he could react, his chair, with him in it, toppled over. An onslaught of wet children surrounded and crawled on him. Another shot of water hit him in the head. He blocked the continuing stream with his hands as Jack let out a whoop.

Keaton exploded with laughter. The children had teamed up against him. Fair enough, he'd put their comradeship to the test. He righted himself and reached for the closet child. It was Clara. Her continuous giggles were like a baby doll's. She threw her arms around his neck as he ran after Bradley. He caught him around the middle and pursued Samantha. His arms were getting full and he didn't have a plan.

He ran too close to the foot-deep wading pool, and Jack shoved him in. He fell backwards into the cool water but balanced the children in his arms so no one got hurt. The thick fabric of his work uniform clung to him with greedy suction while the children laughed uncontrollably. Even Lindsey, who had begun to scold them, couldn't speak for laughing.

She pulled wet children off him before offering a hand to Keaton. If it weren't for the happiness radiating in her gaze, he'd have pulled her in with him.

Lucy joined them and slapped a hand on his wet back. "Looks like we all need to head to the farm. You can change, and Mom's fixed us dinner."

Lindsey paled. Her laughter vanished. "What? I thought you were going to put the roast on?"

"I conveniently forgot. I really like you, Linds, and so will our folks."

Lindsey's look of shock struck a nerve in Keaton. "Lucy, you should've asked first."

Her bobbed blond hair bounced as she spoke. "Why, so I could hear her tell me no? Huh—uh. I like this gal." She looped an arm through Lindsey's and pulled her toward the house.

Keaton followed after them. He wanted to be gentle with Lindsey, not scare her away by throwing her in the midst of his family. "Lindsey, you don't have to—"

"It's okay, Keaton. I can do this." Her confident words couldn't mask the obvious uncertainty in her eyes. He'd just been given a chance to earn her trust by the bank refusing to help, the stress of meeting his parents so soon could jeopardize everything.

Lucy helped the children change and everyone was ready in ten minutes. She grabbed her purse. "Who's riding with me?"

Several shouts of, "Me," responded, which left Clara and Samantha with Keaton and Lindsey. She looked at Keaton, her gaze still uncertain. "I guess I'll drive so I can get everyone home."

"Or, I could leave my rig here and drive your van. That way you won't have to come home to a dark house by yourself." Her shoulders relaxed. He'd said the right thing.

Though he would've never pictured himself behind the wheel of a mini-van before, this would make the second time. But if it meant being a part of this family, he could drive anything. Two little hands grasped his and pulled him toward the van, the girls were as anxious to see his farm as the rest of the children.

He buckled them in and turned back to the house in search of Lindsey. Had she forgotten something? Surely she wasn't having second thoughts. Her other children were already gone with Lucy. He stepped through the door. Lindsey stood with the phone in her hand, her other trembling as she signaled for Keaton to wait.

He fisted his hand in anger. No way was he waiting. Whoever this was needed to know Lindsey wasn't alone. With two long strides, he grasped the phone from Lindsey's hand. "Who is this," he demanded.

A wicked chuckle sounded on the other end. "Ah, the burly boyfriend wants to play, too? So be it. Lindsey can fill you in."

Keaton stared at Lindsey as the disconnected call drummed in his ear. "What did he say?"

Lindsey turned toward the door. "The girls are in the car. We need to go." She slipped outside.

She'd have to tell him. She would tell him. He strode to the back of the house and double-checked the lock. The air conditioner was on and all the windows were still locked. He moved to the front porch and pulled the door closed. He wiggled the knob. It locked tight behind him. Until Lindsey was ready to talk, this was as much as he could do. He prayed it would be enough.

***

Lindsey's stomach rolled with anxiety. The money hadn't been enough to satisfy Clayton. But there was nothing more she could do. The children were already eating staples, like oatmeal for breakfast and beans for dinner, several times a week. The only change that would make enough difference would be to turn off the air conditioner, and that would be misery.

She swiped sweat from her forehead. Missouri summers were never gentle, and they would all miss the comfort of a cooled home. Keaton reached over and squeezed her hand. One glance his direction reminded her Clayton wasn't the only reason for her churning insides.

Meeting Keaton's parents shouldn't cause her such worry. They weren't dating. They were friends, the same as she and Lucy were friends. Right?

No.

Keaton had kissed her. He'd also made it perfectly clear he wanted to be a permanent part of her family. Who was she kidding?

She had every right to be nervous. *Lord, please don't let his parents be like Mike and Donna.* That would be asking too much.

Keaton pulled up to a white farm house situated across the road from his parents' log-cabin. He reached over and clasped her hands. "Relax. There's no rush to meet my folks. I want to show you my house, first."

She moved to open her door, Keaton touched her arm. "Wait, I'll get that."

Samantha hollered from the back seat, "I want out. I want out."

Keaton looked in the rearview mirror and smiled. "Be patient. I have to open the door for your mother first."

"Isn't that a bit old fashioned?" Though the thought made her tingle a bit, Mike had never opened a door for her–ever.

Keaton shrugged. "It may be, but that's how I was taught. And if my mama peeks out the window and sees you getting out on your own, I'll never hear the end of it."

Lindsey laughed and pulled her hand away from the door handle. Samantha started her chant again. She often became so energized Lindsey would lose control of her. She found the best thing for the hyper child was to let her run her energy off.

As Keaton walked around the van, Lindsey turned toward the back. "Samantha, when we get out, I want you to show Keaton how many times you can run around the van, okay?"

"No."

"Samantha," Lindsey hoped she could sway her into this. It would make the rest of the evening far more bearable. "You've never shown him how fast you run. If you don't show him, I'll ask Bradley to instead."

"I do it, I do it!"

Lindsey smiled with relief and turned as Keaton opened her door. "Thank you."

Her gaze dropped to her blue-jean cut-offs and bare legs. "Oh no, I was so busy getting the kids changed, I forgot to."

Keaton's mouth pulled into a slow smile. "I'm glad you didn't. You look great in those."

"Keaton." Irritation mixed with pleasure from his compliment. "I would rather have presented myself a little better than this."

Giggles, mixed with a, "yoo-hoo," sounded from across the road. Lindsey turned to see her children and Lucy, along with what she presumed were his parents, coming toward them. Her gaze fell on his mother. Although they stopped just below her knees, she also sported cut-offs.

Keaton whispered, "You'll fit right in." His arm brushed against her as he stepped past to the sliding door to let the girls outs.

The girls–her mind had concentrated on everything but them, and they were probably more than ready to get out. Keaton handed a sleepy Clara over and jumped back as an energized Samantha shot out of the van.

"Watch how fast me run, Keaton!"

He laughed as she took off around the van, one, two, three, four times before she tired.

Lindsey hoped the old stand-by would work. Sweat trickled down her spine, more from nerves than the August heat. *August already, where did July go?* The thought was disturbing. Two months were catching up quick.

Lucy bounded beside her, smiling. "Linds, these are our folks, Ann and Jacob."

Lindsey reached out to shake hands but was instead embraced by their mother. When Ann pulled back, tears shone in her eyes.

"I'm getting sappy the older I get. We're so happy to meet you." She squeezed Lindsey's hand before Clara made an uncharacteristic lunge into Ann's arms. She held the child close and looked back at Lindsey. "You fit right in, just like your kids."

Fit right in . . . that's what Keaton had said only moments ago.

Jacob stepped forward and patted her arm. "We're glad to have you." Though his words weren't many, his eyes conveyed the same message as his wife's.

Keaton placed a warm hand in the slope of her back and guided her toward the house.

Jack shouted, "We get to see your house?"

Everyone followed together as cheerful voices filled the air. It was as if a Norman Rockwell painting sprang to life. Chickens milled about in the yard not far from their coop. A lazy hound lay stretched out on the porch. And a heavenly blue sky hung above them.

Lindsey stepped onto the front porch and waited for Keaton to swing open the screen-door.

She stepped through and the solid hard-wood door closed behind her. She turned around. She and Keaton were alone. "What are you doing?"

"You get to see it first. The kids can see the goats then get their turn inside."

She didn't understand, but one glance from the window told her everything was okay. Smiles lit everyone's faces as they walked around the house and disappeared from view.

Keaton stood waiting . . . and smiling. His charming slanted eyebrows made her doubt she'd ever grow tired of looking at him. "What do you think of the first room? I'm afraid none of the rooms in this old house are very big."

"It's beautiful." A light smell of varnish permeated the air. The way the oak floor shone, she assumed it'd been recently recoated. The room may not have been as large as some living rooms, but it would be big enough for the family and still lend a cozy atmosphere.

Big enough for the family? She cleared her throat, thankful they were only thoughts and not something she'd said out loud.

"Would you like to see upstairs?"

She turned to see stairs lining the side of the wall. Keaton waved his hand for her to go first. His eyes had a peculiar shine to them. He couldn't have read her thoughts, could he?

The upper story contained two bedrooms and a small bathroom. The varnish smell had been replaced with that of fresh paint. "Did you just paint this bathroom?"

"Yeah, 'cause I just built it."

The small sink and toilet were tucked in a tiny spot beneath the eaves of the roof. Lindsey furrowed her brow. "Why?"

His silence made her turn and face him. She softened at the sweet look on his face—timid hopefulness. A rush of feelings overwhelmed her and made her heart beat faster. He'd built this bathroom for her kids. She didn't need to hear him say it. His expression said it all. Without further thought, she tipped forward and kissed him right on the lips.

"Thank you, Keaton." Lindsey turned and descended the stairs before the reality of her actions settled in.

She'd kissed him.

What had possessed her to do such a thing? *Because you want him. You want to accept his gifts, his warmth, his love.*

A hand slipped around hers and Keaton was by her side, urging her to explore the other side of the house. They came upon a bathroom, thankfully larger than the one upstairs, complete with a shower and tub.

Next, they stepped inside his bedroom. A worn lone-star quilt covered a bed that flanked the side of the wall facing the morning sun. Keaton pulled her toward a door. It opened onto the covered porch that wrapped around the front and side of the house.

Her gaze snuck back to the bed, the bed she would share with Keaton if they married. A combination of nervousness and excitement danced inside. It had been so long since she looked forward to being held by a man.

She felt Keaton's gaze and wanted to crawl in a hole. Shame for her thoughts heated her face before the noise of children saved her from further embarrassment.

Keaton smiled, "Our time's up."

She followed him into the kitchen where everyone gathered. Ann was at the kitchen sink with a chair, instructing the washing of hands.

"Mom, you can pet the chickens! They'll stop beside you and stand still wanting to be petted." Elizabeth's green eyes sparkled with life.

Lindsey directed her outspoken thought to Keaton. "I've never heard of chickens you could pet."

His sheepish shrug was explained by Lucy. "He's a big softy for any animal. He babie's his chickens as much as people do their babies."

"Little sisters," Keaton shook his head toward Lucy, "have big mouths."

Keaton gave the children a quick tour of his home before they all crossed the road to his parents' cabin. Excitement and hopefulness lingered in the air. This family's warm welcome blessed her soul. It was as if she were in a dream.

Then reality struck.

Bradley spilled sticky juice all over the floor. Samantha spewed forth insults over the sight of peas. And Clara had an accident in her pants. It was hard to dream of fairytales with six children around. But Keaton's family didn't mind. His mother took care of Clara, Lucy mopped the floor and their dad agreed with Samantha's opinion of peas.

After dinner, Lindsey helped Ann clean up then it was time to take the kids home to bed. "Thank you for dinner, Ann. And for your patience."

Ann hugged her tight. "It was great to have you."

Keaton held the door open as the children said good night then helped direct them toward the van. It was impossible to overlook how well they fit together. The children responded to his guidance as if he was already their dad and Lindsey accepted his presence with equal ease.

On the way home, the van fell silent with sleepy children. It had been a full day, full of unexpected turns. If she'd been warned of meeting Keaton's parents, she'd have never gotten out of bed. Thankfully she had, or she'd have never known her wishful childhood image of a family truly did exist.

"Want to tell me about your phone call?" Keaton's voice startled her thoughts.

"No."

"Lindsey," a deep sigh followed, "whatever's going on, I can help. Keep in mind I'll be protecting the kids, too."

She fidgeted with her fingers. "This may not be right, but I want a chance to do things on my own. Mike didn't think I had a brain in my head. I want to prove I do."

"Prove to who, Lindsey? Mike's dead."

She swallowed against the building tears in her throat. "Me."

She didn't expect Keaton to understand, nor did she possess the courage to tell him. After years of being told she wasn't good enough or smart enough, she'd stopped believing in herself. She didn't know if she had the intelligence it took to survive on her own or not, but she at least wanted a chance to find out.

Once the children were settled for the night, Lindsey and Keaton again shared the outside swing. This time Keaton held her hand. The soft rumble of his voice tickled her ear. "Are you nervous?"

"No."

"You should be." His voice deepened. "Tonight, I expect a good-night kiss."

Lindsey laughed and tried to scoot away. Keaton only pulled her closer before becoming serious. "Care to share your thoughts about today?"

She cleared her throat. "I haven't had time to process them for myself."

"Chicken," he teased.

"I'm not a chicken."

His voice turned softer. "I'll share mine . . . if you think you can handle it."

Chapter Nine

Keaton didn't wait for her answer. "Seeing you in my house made it feel like home for the first time."

He rubbed his thumb across the back of her hand. "I knew you were the one from the moment I saw you at the fair."

"I remember."

Keaton peered through the moonlight to meet her gaze. "You remember meeting me, two years ago?"

"Didn't we jump ahead of you in line?"

"Yeah." Curiosity gnawed at him. "But why do you remember that?"

Lindsey pulled her hand away from his and tossed her hair over one shoulder, freeing it from between her back and the swing. "You're not easy to forget."

He still didn't understand why, and the look on his face must have conveyed that.

"You're incredibly handsome, Keaton. Surely you've been told that plenty of times before."

Her ending words held a jealous twinge, tickling him with satisfaction. "Never, at least by someone that meant anything to me."

Keaton stood and pulled her in front of him confident she wouldn't turn away. He wrapped his arms around her and lowered his head. "I love you, Lindsey."

Before she could respond, he trapped her lips in his. Like a captured dove, her supple mouth fluttered beneath his before relaxing in safe assurance.

He loved the way she fit in his arms, as if she were made for him. Would she come to see that? Having gotten this close, he couldn't bear the thought of her not marrying him now. He ended their kiss and stepped back. Without another word, he led her to the door of the house. "I'll see you tomorrow. Maybe we can have that hotdog roast we'd planned."

Lindsey nodded in agreement though she still looked confused. Had their kiss caused that? She needed time alone with her thoughts, that much was clear. He placed a kiss on her forehead and opened the door for her to enter. "I'll wait to hear the lock."

***

Lindsey leaned against the kitchen sink. Had he really said he loved her? Goosebumps tickled their way along her arm and neck, raising tiny hairs in excitement. A smile stretched across her face, despite the fact she was the only one in the room.

She pictured Keaton's house and mentally toured each room. The kitchen would be so easy to work in. Large enough to move about and still include a dining table, exactly what she'd always wanted. And the painted plywood cabinets, that towered taller than hers, added a country-warmth making her think of chicken and dumplings and home-made biscuits.

Stifling a yawn, Lindsey knew she should be in bed. The children were already asleep and it was getting late. Reaching her room, she flipped on the light and moved across the floor to her bed. The covering pulled a sigh from her. Old and tattered, the store-bought comforter needed replaced. A quilt like Keaton's would be lovely.

The thought of him sent flutters to her stomach. Shaking off all the reasons she shouldn't want the arranged marriage, Lindsey freed her imagination. Lying across the bed, she daydreamed what it would be like to wake up to Keaton, spend the day with him, and end the day together. His voice resounded in her mind, his lips lingered on hers.

Her conscience begged for honesty.

Part of her hoped she'd have to marry him. They were so compatible, and each day she hungered more for his friendship. And more recently, at night, she dreamed of him beside her.

Was it wrong to think like this so soon after burying her husband? She couldn't remember the last time Mike had shown her affection. Cancer was a parasite, a thief of emotion. She paused. The truth creased her brow. Her marriage had lost its vitality long before disease had entered the picture. It had never been a fairytale romance, even from the beginning.

***

Keaton returned in the morning for another fun day. He really did love her. Otherwise, the man would stop coming around. A child was always hanging on him, or wiping a dirty hand on his shirt. There always seemed to be a spill or an 'owie' to deal with, not to mention the children had tried to drown him in the wading pool.

Yet, he was willing to take them back to the water today.

Elizabeth's voice startled her from her thoughts. "Mom, it's for you."

Lindsey turned to accept the phone. She hadn't even heard it ring. "Hello?"

"Lindsey, this is your mother-in-law, Donna."

Silence hovered in the air as Lindsey waited for her to continue. She found her own voice and filled the gap. "Hi, Donna. How are you?"

"We're all fine. I'm curious how you're doing." Another awkward moment followed before Donna continued. "And please don't tell me you're fine. I want details."

"Why?" The innocent question left her lips before she could stop it. What need would she have for details? Did she plan to use them against her? Could Clayton have been so clever he would contact them to build his case? Lindsey shook her head. No. Clayton was a drug user, he couldn't be smart enough to—

"Lindsey, are you still there?"

"Sorry, Donna." Her mother-in-law's impatience demanded her attention. "I'm not sure what it is you want to know. We're still in the same predicament we were when you last saw us."

"Are you still planning on marrying that man?" She cleared her throat. "Elizabeth seems quite fond of him."

Donna must have spoken with Elizabeth before asking for her. Lindsey worried her lip. What had her daughter said?

"It seems," Donna's voice cracked, "the children have already replaced my son—their father. What's wrong with you, Lindsey?"

Lindsey batted against tears of rage. She didn't sign up for this. This was Mike's fault. Resentment settled in the pit of her stomach. "I tried to talk to you and Michael, Donna. I wanted help. You didn't offer it."

"Actually, we did." Donna's voice held a sweet sarcasm. "Are your nieces still living with you?"

Lindsey's hand dropped from her ear. She stared at the offending phone now held in front of her. Her finger itched to press the off button. Whatever reason Donna had for calling, it wasn't out of true concern for her or the children. If she truly wanted to help the kids, she wouldn't send two of them away.

Her thumb hovered over the red button . . . but she couldn't do it. Church had taught her to respect her elders. To hang up would be rude. With a heavy heart, she drew the phone to her ear.

"Donna?" A disconnected signal drummed in her ear. Donna had hung up on her.

The urge to cry welled inside her like flood waters pressing against a dam. As if the home she'd grown up in hadn't been bad enough, she'd lost her sister, mother, and husband . . . and never felt loved by any of them. On top of all that, her in-laws made her feel unworthy, unintelligent, unwanted, the list could go on. Pressure pushed against her eyes and settled like a ball in her forehead. She rubbed the forming headache and swiped at escaping tears.

A paper verse propped on her windowsill came into focus. One of the ladies from church had taped it on top of a casserole. *Trust in the Lord with all thine heart; and lean not unto thine own understanding. In all thy ways acknowledge him, and he shall direct thy paths.*

Lindsey bowed her head to pray.

"Mom! I had the ball first, and Bradley took it."

This is what her life had become. Now a single mother, she had to fight every battle on her own. Even the battle to pray. She sighed as she turned to settle the fight.

After a couple books were read, laundry changed, and bedrooms picked up, Lindsey returned to the kitchen to prepare lunch. She withdrew the items for a chicken salad from the refrigerator. The celery and mayonnaise were easy to find given the sparse interior. She needed to shop for groceries again, but having given money to Clayton, she didn't have much left over.

She turned the water on at the sink to wash the celery. The well water cooled her body temperature as it ran over her wrists. Outside the kitchen window, Lindsey watched Keaton mow around a plant that had grown in the middle of the yard. Why didn't he just mow it down? They didn't have any flowers planted there. She waited until he and Jack finished and met him outside. "Keaton, what is that?" She pointed toward the plant.

Keaton dipped his head in that enduring shy boy look he so often made and glanced up beneath slanted brows. "It's a flower. Actually, it's Butterfly Milkweed. Give it a few more days and it'll be full of small orange blossoms and loaded with butterflies."

He slid his thumbs in his back pockets and nodded toward the house. "You'll be able to watch them from the kitchen window."

His thoughtfulness pierced through her remaining defenses. Her heart swelled with love for him. Lindsey blinked back tears as they misted her eyes and returned her gaze to the flower. Her heart had never spun this way for any man before. How could she know if her feelings were love or appreciation? When she and Mike had met, his interest excited her, but goose-bumps had *never* followed his touch. His words of freedom were what had won her hand. *"I'll get you out of here."*

Mike had been a good father, but he'd failed *miserably* as a husband. He took care of her only if she obeyed. When she did anything to upset him, his punishment was a harsh tongue, reminding her how incompetent she was. Though he'd never raised a hand against her she'd often wished he would, at least it would be over. But his words carried a lasting effect, robbing her self-worth, fading her identity.

Her eldest son caught up with her in the yard, his leg brushing against the milkweed as he hurried past. The only flowers Mike had ever given her had been for their wedding day. Was God so merciful He'd grant her both a good father *and* husband in Keaton? She wished for a clear, booming answer from above.

Keaton followed her into the house and helped the boys gather their swimming gear while she helped the girls. Once the children and food were loaded, they headed down the gravel road to the river access.

The two oldest children rode on the tail-gate of the Bronco while everyone else crowded inside. Clara insisted sitting on Keaton's lap. He accepted her presence with gentle ease, driving with one hand on the wheel and one loosely wrapped around the toddler's middle. Bradley occupied Lindsey's lap while the other two sat in the small back seat.

The smell of the river reached her senses before it came into view and brought with it flashbacks of earlier years. Before the addition of their youngest and her nieces, Mike had made time for the children. At least once a month he'd do something special, such as take them out for ice cream, or if weather permitted, a dunk in the river. The children had always been thrilled with the added attention.

Keaton pulled the Bronco to a stop beside the river and opened the door. Lindsey followed suit with Bradley in tow, but her mind was elsewhere. Why didn't the thought of Mike make her sad? Shouldn't she miss him, at least a little?

Elizabeth's voice resounded Lindsey's memories. "Dad took us here." She looked back at Keaton and reached for his hand. "I mean, our first dad."

Were all her children ready to move on? She'd insisted they call him, Keaton, but it appeared as though they'd united under a different front.

They reached the bank of the river and Keaton took Clara's hand from hers. "I'll take the first shift."

She stared at him and raised a brow. "What are you talking about?"

"How often do you get to swim, Lindsey?"

A half-laugh rose in her throat. "Never."

"Then I believe it's your turn. Have fun."

Her jaw dropped. She'd never grow tired of this man. Just when she thought he couldn't possibly more considerate, he surprised her again.

Leaning back into the river, Lindsey shivered as water slowly trickled into her ears muting the sounds of the river's occupants. She moved her arms back and forth and floated with the slow current. It had been far longer than she could remember since she'd felt so relaxed. The lazy water lapped at her temples lulling her into a dreamy state.

She opened her eyes. Overhanging trees parted to expose blue sky dotted with puffy, white clouds. Her breath stalled at the beauty bestowed by the Master Creator, all light and color working together in a perfect visual symphony.

Thank you, God, for the peace You've given me right now. Help me to always hold onto it and use it when things turn stressful.

Jack's laughter became recognizable even through the water. She'd had her fun, now she needed to return and help Keaton. This was the first time in her life she'd ever felt comfortable leaving her children in care of another. Keaton and his family had won her trust with effortless ease.

"Hey."

Lindsey forced her feet to the bed of the river and stood up. She'd bumped into a child snorkeling. "Sorry. I wasn't paying attention."

The child shrugged and dove under again. Lindsey noted the distance back to her family and began a breast stroke in their direction, enjoying the cleansing power of exertion.

***

Keaton kept a constant head count on the children. A popular spot, the river attracted a large crowd during the summer months. Not only did he and Lindsey need to keep to shallow water, they also had to keep the children from wandering off with other kids.

Lindsey moved a chair to a shady spot near the bank to keep Clara from getting too much sun. The child's pale skin made her susceptible to sunburn, even through sunblock. He pulled his gaze from Lindsey long enough to count the children and reward Jack with a return splash before his eyes trailed back to her.

She'd mentioned Mike didn't often take her anywhere. It was no wonder. Her beauty captured everyone's attention. Although there were plenty of young women in two-piece swimwear, they couldn't compare to the graceful woman in her full-piece swimsuit. Accented by the suit's bright blue color, the summer sun had turned her milky skin into a warm brown.

If the other women's glares were any indication, he doubted Lindsey had many friends. His sister Lucy could make up for that. Since she'd been through a similar situation, she and Lindsey had already formed a close bond.

A child yelled.

Keaton spun around and found Josh trying to shake something from his hand. He waded to his side to see a craw-dad hanging on with one pincher.

"Get it off. Please, Dad, get it off!" His face twisted in pain.

Dad. Keaton's heart twisted.

"Hold still, I'll have it off in a jif."

Josh wriggled and moaned. "It really hurts."

Something brushed against Keaton's foot. He glanced down. His foot stood in a dam near the bank that the boys had built. Inside were numerous other craw-dads clambering to get out. He jumped back before one decided to snap at him. He forced the pincher to open and held the craw-dad up for Josh to see, careful to keep his own fingers away from the pinchers.

Aside from Lindsey and the children, they'd drawn a slight crowd. A familiar voice spoke above the excited chatter of children. He looked up to see a fellow employer, Doug Whitaker.

The man took a swig from the can he held, the pungent odor reeking of cheap alcohol. "I'm here with my family and kinfolk. Who are you here with, *Dad*?" His sardonic smile said he already knew.

Although Keaton's gaze wanted to slide to Lindsey, he held it on Doug. "Same." He turned to leave as the children dispersed with their mom, but Doug grabbed his arm.

"Now I understand why you're playing saint. She's Heaven's reward in the flesh." He took another swig. "Shucks, she could tempt anyone."

Keaton balled his hands into fists and spoke in a low, clear tone. "You'd best get back to your family, Doug."

Doug pulled his eyes from Lindsey and smiled at Keaton. Nothing else was said, but the message was clear. Lindsey's reputation was stained. Not only did Doug have the wrong idea, but he'd share it with whoever would listen.

Keaton took in the river scene. People dotted every shore and water hole. The attraction was gone. Too many people, too many opinions. He waded across to Lindsey and the kids. "Let's get in the Bronco. I know a better spot to swim. The water's not as wide, but there's less people."

Josh rubbed his hand. "Are there crawl-dads?"

Keaton couldn't help smiling at the boy's term. "Not as many."

Against a few protests by the children, they climbed back into his vehicle and took a different route. Ten minutes later, Keaton pulled onto a beaten path that led to a quiet water hole.

Lindsey took in the serene atmosphere. "This is perfect."

"Well, there's not a spot deep enough for *us* to swim, but we don't need one. It's just right for the kids."

The children ran in front of them and resumed their water games with enthusiasm. Keaton pulled Lindsey to a stop a few yards from hearing distance. He still hadn't been able to rid Doug from his mind. "Lindsey, I didn't think about…" He scratched his head and looked away.

"I know."

"You know?"

Lindsey nodded. "There'll be rumors." She stepped toward a tree and slid down to watch the kids at play. "I haven't told my church even."

"That you plan to marry—" The hope was quick and strong.

"No." Lindsey shook her head. "I mean about Mike's plans. I still–I don't know about anything else."

The sensitive subject made them both uncomfortable. Keaton picked up a broken twig and doodled in the sand. His eyes trailed to the children, all six of them. They laughed, splashed, fought and laughed some more. He loved them. He loved their mother. And he wouldn't give up on making them his own.

Keaton rose and dusted off. "I'll get a fire going for s'mores."

"You mean hotdogs first, right?"

He grinned and shook his head. "No, my family eats their marshmallows first."

"But . . ."

His smile faded as he waited for her to object. He'd referred to his family, not hers. But this one *would* be his family, if she'd only let him. Lindsey's mouth slowly closed.

Keaton could breathe again.

The s'mores were a big hit. They would all need to wash off in the river before eating hotdogs, otherwise the buns would stick to their fingers. Keaton watched Lindsey from across the flames. They'd stationed themselves apart to keep watch over the children. Sticky marshmallow matted a section of hair over her shoulder from where Clara had reached for her. She'd grimaced as she tried to pull it out of Clara's hand, but otherwise laughed it off. Her patience astounded him.

Jack popped his last allowed marshmallow into his mouth and tried to whistle. This caused an eruption of giggles.

Just as quickly, Elizabeth stopped laughing. "I remember Daddy doing that."

The children fell silent. Lindsey looked from one to the other. But what was she thinking? Keaton cleared his throat. "What else did he do?"

Josh spoke up. "He told us stories."

"Yeah, about bears and other animals he'd hunt!" Jack waved his roasting stick in the air. "One time he had to fight off a bear that attacked their camp."

The children relished in the memories of their father's hunting trips while Lindsey withdrew into a faraway silence, making Keaton more curious.

***

Keaton pulled into Lindsey's driveway and looked at the sleepy children in the back seat. It'd been a fun day for them. He accepted the house keys from Lindsey and strolled to the door. The air conditioner's hum sounded more like a car engine than a cooling unit. He didn't remember it being so loud.

The dead-bolt turned over, and he stepped inside. Despite the familiar surroundings, a strange eeriness hovered in the air.

"Why's the air conditioner so loud?" Lindsey's voiced startled him. He hadn't realized she stood behind him.

"Did you leave a window open? It sounds like it's pulling."

"No . . ." Her voice faded as she passed around him with hesitant steps.

Across the room, Keaton saw the reason for alarm. A whole window pane lay shattered on the floor. His heart quickened as he stepped forward to stop Lindsey. He bumped into her. She'd stopped in mid-stride. Had she seen it too?

"Keaton," his name quivered from her lips. Lindsey held a shaky finger toward the table. "What's that?"

"Candy, yeah!" Jack raced by in excitement. Keaton and Lindsey each caught his arm and pulled him back.

"Lindsey, keep the kids in the living room." Keaton moved to the table, careful not to mar anything with fingerprints. Centered on top of the table sat a candy arrangement typical of what one would find at a hospital gift shop. He flipped open his pocketknife and opened the folded card with its blade.

For my girls.

Love,

Daddy

Chapter Ten

Lindsey gathered the children on the sofa with instructions to remain seated. Samantha whined and begged for a movie.

Was Clayton the cause of the broken window and the candy? She knew he was. During his last phone call he had all but admitted his plan.

"Lindsey." He'd breathed her name into the receiver with chilling familiarity. "It'd be so easy to get one of your young'uns hooked. You wouldn't want them share'n my habit, would ya? I bet my girls would take right to it."

He'd emitted a nasty laugh. "I need money, Sis."

Keaton had grabbed the phone from her hand before anything else was said.

"Movie! Movie!" Lindsey jumped at the sound of Samantha and Bradley's chime.

She cleared her thoughts and moved toward the cabinet in search of something to hold their interest.

"Lindsey, don't touch anything." Keaton was at her side. "My cell's in the truck. Let's load the kids in your van and I'll call this in."

Jack took his brothers' hands and moved to the door in obedience. "Will you tell us what's wrong?"

Lindsey watched Keaton place a hand on her son's shoulder. "Later. Right now, I'd appreciate you helping us get everyone buckled in."

Jack stood straighter and nodded his head as he took charge of his siblings.

***

Lindsey stepped back against the van as a huge, red dog plodded up to her, insistent on making his presence known. "A hunting dog."

She vaguely remembered a dog on the porch last time she visited but hadn't given it any thought.

Keaton stepped around his bronco and lengthened his stride to snag the dog's collar. "Sorry, Samson wouldn't hurt a flea."

She could only nod and slide along the van to open the sliding door. She eyed the pair behind her to make sure Keaton still remained in control of the large animal.

Mike's hunting dogs were still boarded at his friend's. She hoped he kept them. She resented everything connected with his time-consuming sport.

The children slid out of the van in an excited frenzy and raced one another to the farmhouse door. Lindsey looked after them with relief. Their happiness eased her worry about their reaction to the break-in at home.

Keaton had chained the dog and now stood with a curious gaze. If he was trying to discern her thoughts, he'd have to wait. Heavier matters were at hand. She squared her shoulders and heaved a full breath. "I guess it's time to head back to my house."

Lindsey saw the door open and Ann waved from the porch. "I've got the kids, you two run along and settle up with the police."

The police. Since when did her life include those words?

***

"Lindsey, why didn't you tell me?" Keaton tightened his grip on the steering wheel. Frustration gnawed at his stomach. The police had provided very little information, while it seemed Lindsey had much more to offer.

Keaton watched her eyes fill with tears before she blinked to hold them at bay. She worried her hands and finally shoved them through her hair. She wanted to tell him, that much was clear, but he suspected fear kept her silent. What did she have to fear from him?

"Lindsey, you can trust me."

Her lips quivered before she covered them with her fingers. "I've never been able to trust anyone, Keaton. Why should I think you're any different?"

The blow of her words struck him in the chest. He'd never had anyone doubt his sincerity, definitely not his trustworthiness. How could he convince her? Was it even possible? Their relationship couldn't continue if she wouldn't— or couldn't— believe in him.

He shrugged his defeated shoulders. "I don't know how to convince you, Lindsey, any further than what I've shown you the past few weeks."

He fell silent for a moment. "Do you trust God?"

"Yes."

Somehow the answer didn't bring comfort like he'd hoped. She knew how to trust God, just not him. An ache throbbed where his heart should've been. Numb fingers turned the ignition over and he continued toward home. Maybe this was it. He'd fixed up the farmhouse to welcome a family he couldn't keep.

All right, God, I can't make sense out of this one. If there's a lesson to be learned, please help me see it and fast. 'Cause all I can tell from here is that I waited for years to have a family because of the woman seated beside me, and now it looks like I can't have her after all.

Keaton knew he'd have his head in the Bible tonight. Scripture often held the answers his prayers sought. Of course he might be up all night reading; he wasn't one to quit without a fight.

Silence suffocated them the rest of the drive home. Rather than force conversation, Keaton used the extra time to mentally organize the facts. Facts that, up until tonight, had been kept from him.

Clayton Turnbaugh had been contacting Lindsey since the day of the funeral, wanting money. Money to fuel his drug addiction. Two things made Keaton's insides curl. One, the low-life had the audacity to threaten the safety of the children. Two, Lindsey had already given him money. Which meant he would continue to harass her for more.

Lindsey's hand reached for the door as soon as his house came into view. Was she that eager to escape him, or did she just want to see her kids? Keaton met her at the front of the Bronco. She hadn't waited for him to open the door. "I'm sure the kids are fine. My dad's probably here, too."

A nod was all she afforded him. The door opened with his dad standing aside, waving them in. "Mom's waiting in the kitchen with coffee, the kids are all in their sleeping bags upstairs."

Lindsey lifted her eyes to the stairs. "Already?"

Jacob chuckled. "They were eager to *camp out*."

Lindsey gave a half-smile before stepping toward the stairs. "I'll just look in on them before I join you."

Keaton followed his dad into the kitchen and slumped in a chair. His mother sat quietly as he rubbed his hands over his temples and through his hair. He was sure she had questions but they needed to wait for Lindsey. Although he was behind her all the way, this was more her fight than his. It wouldn't be right to share more than she wanted.

His mother held a cup of coffee toward her as she joined them at the table. "What did the police say?"

Lindsey glanced at Keaton and back to her cup. "You didn't tell them already?"

He only shook his head. Why would she expect him to? He felt a curtain of knowledge pull back. Mike ran the show in their relationship, in every possible way. Of course she would expect Keaton to have taken control of the conversation. Her lack of trust was beginning to make sense.

Thanks to Mike, he had a tough month ahead of him.

Lindsey cleared her throat. "The police said they'd dust the candy for prints, but that was all they could do."

"Did they search for foot-prints? Surely whoever did this left a hint somewhere?" Jacob's frustration was evident. Keaton admired his dad for his concern. "I thought of that and told the police they might want to at least try to get prints from the shards of glass. They nodded their heads as though it was a good idea, but didn't comment."

The evening ended with Keaton and Lindsey on the porch watching as his parents crossed the road to their cabin. He'd soon join them, and give the house to Lindsey and the kids for the night, maybe for the week, depending on the situation at her house.

Thoughts of the evening cluttered his mind, too many to try to give credence to now. Instead, Keaton swung around to face Lindsey.

He reached for her hand, she didn't pull away. "Keep the door locked." When their eyes met, her chocolate gaze reflected her inner turmoil.

Keaton acted on impulse and drew her into his embrace. She stiffened, but only for a moment before relaxing against his chest. "What I told you the other night still stands. Good night, Lindsey." He turned away and strode toward the road. One look back told him she hadn't moved. Her lone figure stood in the pale light of the porch. He refused to look back again. If he did, he knew he wouldn't be able to leave.

***

The following morning, Lindsey greeted Keaton with detached warmth. Though the thought made her want to cry, she had to keep him at arm's-length. He confused her to the extent of craziness. He doted over her and the children with a tenderness she longed for, but if he was a hunter, he'd turn out just like Mike. She couldn't trust her heart to another man like that. And definitely not her children's hearts.

She watched her children follow Keaton and Jacob, excited at the chance to do farm-work. Even Clara had insisted she go by reaching for Keaton and mouthing a silent word. Lindsey didn't want to admit it, but it seemed the child wanted to say, "Da-da." If all her children expected him to be their dad, they weren't going to make it easy on her when she didn't let it happen.

She glanced down at the dog splayed across the top porch step. He lifted his pointed head and stretched his jaw wide in a lazy yawn. Tears misted her eyes. The dog had ruined it for her. By his coloring and build, he looked like a pure-bred redbone. Nobody would keep an expensive hunting dog without good reason. Did Mike choose Keaton because of common interests they'd shared? *Did they ever go on a trip together?* The thought sent ice through her veins, but she didn't remember Mike ever mentioning Keaton being on one of his *vacations*.

The animal laid his head back with a huge sigh then rolled blood-shot eyes in her direction. "Don't expect me to pet you. You stand for everything I don't like."

"Who, Samson?" Lucy's clear voice surprised her.

Happiness at her presence brought a smile to her face. She hadn't expected to see her new friend. "Hi, I'm glad you're here."

"What are you taking out on this spoiled mutt?" Lucy climbed the porch, stepping over the hound, to join Lindsey on the swing.

"Mutt? I thought he was a pure-bred."

Lucy shrugged her shoulders. "He probably is, but he never pulls any weight around here so I call him a mutt." She moved to sit by the dog and roughed up his ears. Samson moaned with pleasure and plopped a huge paw in her lap.

Had she been wrong to be so distant to Keaton? Now she wasn't sure. "Doesn't Keaton use him on hunting trips?"

Lucy snorted. "Ha, Keaton hunt? That brother of mine is more of a Johnny Appleseed. He'd rather train a squirrel than kill one."

"But what does he do for meat?"

Lucy spanned her hand in front of her. "He grows it in the field. We all butcher a cow between us each year. That's what fills our freezers."

Reality of her situation dawned on her. Keaton wasn't like Mike. Yet, she'd pushed him away, accusing him of being untrustworthy. Regret built behind her eyes. Would he forgive her foolishness? She was so confused. Life with Mike made building any relationship a trial. Trust had been an imaginative term. Walls of protection had been an everyday defense.

"Did your husband hunt?"

Lindsey looked up to find Lucy staring at her, probably trying to read her thoughts. "Yes. Every time he earned vacation days, he spent them on huge, expensive hunting trips." If bitterness showed in her voice, she didn't care. She felt she could be honest with Lucy.

"My brother's nothing like Mike, Lindsey. Give him a chance."

She nodded her head in solemn agreement, but it didn't lesson the ball of weight settling in her abdomen. *Lord, please don't let me have messed things up.*

"Have any breakfast left-overs?"

Lindsey appreciated the change of topic. "If you're hungry for pancakes."

Lucy jumped to her feet, startling the dog. "I'm always hungry."

They shared breakfast at the chrome table in the kitchen. Lindsey's nerves settled the more time she spent with Lucy. Their common bond had already forged an unbreakable friendship.

Lucy smiled mischievously. "Is Keaton's bed comfortable?"

Darting her eyes to her plate, Lindsey forked another bite. "I fell asleep on the couch."

"Too bad. You might've had some fun dreams."

"Lucy!" Lindsey stifled a laugh at her friend's boldness and searched for another change of topic. "So tell me, do you date?"

Lucy's aqua eyes widened at the unexpected question. "No. Trying to keep my farm going keeps me too busy to think that way."

"I still can't believe you run a farm on your own. I guess what you lack in size you make up for in gutso."

Lucy giggled. "You mean, gusto."

"Oh, yeah." Lindsey hung her head in mock shame. "I'm always getting words and clichés mixed up. It used to embarrass Mike, but Keaton just laughs and corrects me."

"You guys will make a great family."

Lindsey didn't feel up to discussing that subject. "But you're young, don't you want a family?"

Lucy swallowed and stared into nothing. "I can't consider dating. I know it's been two years, but I don't feel settled." She swiped her hands against her legs. Her constant smile faded as worry lines creased her brow. "It almost feels like . . ."

Concern for her filled Lindsey's heart. This was the first time Lucy had ever shown anything but a positive outlook.

Lucy continued, "Like something isn't finished."

"What isn't finished?"

"Good morning!" Ann called from the front door.

Lucy turned to Lindsey. "Don't repeat this to anyone. Promise?"

Lindsey had no idea what she'd repeat. Lucy hadn't given her any information, still she nodded her head in agreement.

Chapter Eleven

Lunch passed in a flurry of activity. Under Ann's direction, Lindsey and Lucy prepared a full meal that included left-overs for dinner. The children chattered constantly about their morning adventure, stealing Lindsey's chances for a conversation with Keaton.

Ann shooed them outside when it was time to clean-up. "You all enjoy the sunshine. I'll have this done in no time."

While Lucy and Jacob set up a game of croquette, Keaton helped Lindsey clean out her van. Her hand brushed against his as they each grabbed for a sucker stick stuck to the carpet. The familiar jolt shot sparks up her arm. Now was the time to apologize. "Keaton, about yesterday, I wanted to–"

"Keaton." Ann stood on the porch waving a cordless phone. "It's work."

"Be right there." He looked across the open sliding door, regret in his eyes. "I'm sorry, Lindsey. They've been having problems with a robot, I'll be right back."

Lindsey watched him cross the yard and take the call. She knew how much the company valued his knowledge. Even Mike had had a habit of calling on him, often in the middle of the night after he'd received a call. Since Keaton didn't have a family, he'd always been willing to go in so Mike wouldn't have to.

She plopped down on the floor of the van with her knees tucked under her chin. If Keaton was granted Mike's job, he'd be at work more than at home, just like Mike had been. With Mike, she honestly hadn't cared. In fact, the house was always more peaceful in his absence. But Keaton would be missed. *Missed very much.*

"Aunt Lindsey." Samantha crawled after something in the yard, "look at all the hopper-jumpers!"

Lindsey laughed at her misuse of *grasshopper* and joined her on the lawn. "I wouldn't try to catch one if I were you— they can bite."

The funny look on Samantha's face pulled another laugh from Lindsey. Samantha jumped to her feet. "I don't want them bite me!"

"If you don't try to catch them, they won't. Just have fun watching them eat grass. Did you know they can fly, too?"

As if on cue, a grasshopper spread its wings and took flight. Samantha pointed, and jumped up and down, "Lookie, lookie!" She turned toward Lindsey. "Can me call you, Mama? I call him, Daddy."

Lindsey's eyes trailed to where her niece's little finger pointed. Keaton walked toward them dressed for work. She turned back to the cherubic face looking at her in earnest. Her heart squeezed with joy. "Of course you can call me Mama. I would love that."

Samantha squealed, squeezed Lindsey, and ran off to play with her siblings.

"Sorry, I have to go." Keaton paused. "You're staying here, right?"

Lindsey nodded as she accepted his hand to pull her to a stance. They still had to replace the window pane. The plastic that covered it was only meant to keep out the weather, not Clayton.

"I'll pick up the glass while I'm in town." He remained standing in place, as if wanting to kiss her but unsure.

Lindsey tipped forward and placed a gentle kiss on his lips. That made the second time she'd initiated affection. His eyes took on a glow that made the effort completely worth-while.

She watched him leave then returned to the van. It wasn't that her vehicle was very dirty, Mike had taught her to always keep it clean, but she needed the time alone with her thoughts. Maybe she should keep the kids from calling Keaton, *Dad*. But what was the use? There didn't seem to be any other choice than to marry him. Her in-laws would be livid. It shouldn't matter what they thought, since they'd never shown any interest in her, but somehow it did. More importantly though, what would her church family think? She still hadn't told them. She steeled herself in preparation. It had to be done, and soon.

***

Keaton stifled a yawn as he packed away his tools. He'd finally managed to get the machine working properly, although he didn't know how long it would last. The new part wouldn't be in for another two weeks. This made the third time he'd been called in this week for various machine problems. Though a fifty hour work week didn't bother him, sixty hours was pushing it.

More than once, his dad had to check his cattle. Relying on someone else to take care of his responsibilities never set well with him. If he became manager, the problem would only become worse.

His thoughts trailed back to Lindsey, where they never strayed far. The more time they spent together the less he wanted to be apart. Like an oasis in the desert, she brought life to his soul. He'd looked forward to their time alone fixing the window at her house. Work was the last place he wanted to spend his Saturday afternoon.

He envisioned her laughing and covered in bubbles. A smile had made all the difference, it erased the worry and doubt Mike and his parents had created. Though she never spoke about them, he knew her in-laws still brought on stress. What made people so vile they only seemed content when causing discomfort to someone else?

He parked at his parents' cabin glad to be home— well, almost home. At least his mom's couch was comfortable. She'd long since turned the extra bedroom into a sewing room. When his brother, Ethan, and his wife, Carli came to visit, they stayed with him. His siblings knew they were always welcome in their grandparents' house. Of course, once he married Lindsey, it would be a crowded visit, especially with the coming addition of Carli's twins.

The thought of family brought his older sister Emily to mind. She was away on another mission trip and knew very little of what was happening at home. He smiled. She would tease him about being jealous of his kids when she came home. Having always boasted she'd be the first to have children, she and their youngest sibling Lucy were currently tied for last.

He stepped inside as quietly as possible. At two am, he didn't want to wake his parents. He closed the door and heard his father's voice from the living room.

"Get everything in tip—top shape again, Son?"

"I hope. If not, they'll have to call someone else." He was surprised his dad was still up. He must have something on his mind. Keaton removed his boots then took a seat on the couch. "What are you still doing up?"

His dad adjusted the recliner to rest his feet on the floor. "Son, I know you've been vying for a management position for a while, but now's the time to be honest with yourself."

Keaton prepared himself for the coming wisdom. He hoped it confirmed what he'd already been thinking. If not, he'd be more confused than ever.

"Can you really be the father you need to be by working so many hours away from home? I know Lindsey's used to that way of life, but is that what you want for your family?"

Keaton let his father's words take root in his heart. They were a balm to his soul, mirroring his own concerns. He'd always planned to be the same kind of father as the man before him. But he couldn't expect to forge those types of relationships if he was always on call. Not to mention the time he'd lose with Lindsey.

He ran a hand through his hair. "I'd already been giving this some thought and prayer. I guess hearing it from someone else is what I needed."

"Those are some special kids. They need a lot of love. And you need to be there to give it." He chuckled, "Otherwise, they're gonna like their Grandpa Jacob best!"

Keaton said good-night to his dad and stretched out on the worn sofa. Its soft cushions hugged his hips but his shoulders were too wide for the seat. He adjusted to his side and almost drifted off to sleep when his hound barked from across the road.

That's not uncommon. I'm sure it's probably nothing. His thoughts did little to reassure him. He'd never be able to sleep unless he checked on Lindsey and the kids. As quietly as possible, Keaton slipped from the cabin and across the road. Staying in the shadows, he crept around the perimeter of his yard. Samson came up behind him and stuck his cold nose in Keaton's palm, startling him to jump. "Samson, you sneak, I was beginning to wonder what happened to you."

He searched the dark, watching for any movement. An owl hooted in a nearby tree, but otherwise all was quiet. "What got you to barking, boy?"

Samson raised the hair on his neck and gave a low growl as he stalked toward the chicken coop. Keaton followed behind, cautious of everything. Edging to the wooden side of the small outbuilding, something rustled on the opposite end. Samson exploded into barking as a fat opossum lost his balance on the side of the fence and fell to the ground. In a frenzy of movement, the hound clamored for the rodent as it scampered up a tree to safety.

Keaton ran a hand over his face in relief it wasn't something more. He leaned against the coop and stared at the sky. Numerous blinking lights stared back. The Bible said God had named each one. As numerous as the sands in the sea, yet they were important enough to name, then how much more important were His children.

God, I know you're there. I believe Your Word and that You'll never leave us nor forsake us. Please watch over this family. And whether it's selfish or not, please make them mine. He looked toward the house and back to the sky. *That's all I've got for now.*

His prayers had never been eloquent, but He believed God heard every one.

***

Keaton awoke to the muted sound of his rooster. His crow wasn't nearly as deafening from across the road. He stretched lazily until the scent of bacon hit his nostrils. Sitting up, he turned toward the kitchen, his stomach already growling in response.

"Mmm, mmm, but something smells good, Mama."

Ann turned from the stove and smiled at her son. "There's a cup of coffee for you on the table. You'll have to wait your turn for the shower. Dad's in there now."

"Not a problem, I like to start off slowly. Let the caffeine have time to take effect." He settled into a chair at the table.

Ann set a bowl and a carton of eggs in front of him. He began cracking them open as she rolled out biscuits across the table.

"I really like Lindsey and her children."

Keaton smiled and met her gaze, but his breath held at her troubled look. "What's wrong?"

His mother reached to twirl a strand of hair, a habit she always did when something was on her mind. Only this time, one glance at her dough covered fingers and she pulled back. "I'm worried for them is all. I've had some awful dreams. Why won't she just marry you? I can tell she has feelings for you and it would keep them all safe."

Her eyes filled with tears as Keaton moved to her side. He hugged her to him and kissed the top of her head. "It'll all work out, Mom. Have faith, it'll all work out."

With breakfast and his shower finished, Keaton walked across the road to his house. He'd sounded confident enough to his mother, but worry filled his mind.

Jack met him at the door. "Hey, wanna come in my house?" The boy giggled over his joke as he waved his hand toward the living room.

Keaton ruffled his hair and stepped through. He'd never grow tired of these kids. They brought a constant smile to his face. "Where's your Mom—" Lindsey halted outside his bedroom, her face a mask of concern, her hair still rumbled from sleep.

"Keaton, y-you're here."

His smile slowly fell away as caution tensed his frame. "What's wrong, Lindsey?"

Josh appeared by her side, trying to hide behind her legs. "I'm sorry, Dad-dy." An emotional cry followed.

Keaton dropped to the boy's side. "What's wrong, Buddy?'

Josh threw his arms around Keaton's neck. Keaton stood with the boy held close and looked toward Lindsey.

She hung her head. "I'm sorry, please don't be mad. I didn't know he had the lizard in his pocket. I promise you we'll find it. We won't let it die in the house—"

A deep laughter rumbled from his chest. A lizard? They were upset over a lizard? "Lindsey, don't worry about it. Remember, I was a boy once, too." He pulled Josh away from his chest to force their eyes to meet. "You caught a lizard! You must be really fast."

Josh sniffed, all worry gone, and nodded his head with excitement. "And he was this big." He held his fingers a few inches apart.

Lindsey pulled at her lip. "We will find it though. And I'm really sorry."

Keaton stared at her, puzzled. She acted afraid. Afraid of what—his temper? "I'm not upset, Lindsey." This was even worse than he'd assumed. She was scared of him?

He lowered Josh to the floor. "Why don't you look for the lizard in the living room while your mom and I look in here?" Josh nodded in compliance and ran into the other room. Keaton took Lindsey's hand and guided her to the porch off his bedroom.

"Lindsey, I don't get mad."

Her gaze dropped to the floor.

"I want you to trust me. I don't want you to be afraid of me—ever." He held his hands out. "Even if I get annoyed or upset, I would never— ever, do anything or say anything to hurt you. I promise."

Lindsey stepped closer and laid her head on his chest. Quiet sobs followed as he rubbed a hand over her back. What had Mike done?

Chapter Twelve

Lindsey took a step back, embarrassed by her show of emotion. Would she ever accept that Keaton was nothing like Mike? She knew she chanced pushing him away for good if she didn't figure out a way to accept their differences soon. "I'm sorry."

Keaton pulled her close again and covered her mouth with his, cutting off her apology. Still raw with emotion, Lindsey easily succumbed to his warmth and tenderness. She pulled tighter to him, hungry for affection. Aware of his hands holding her fast, she not only felt safe, she felt wanted— an unfamiliar, but welcome, feeling. He left her lips, leaving a scent of mint from his breath, and sought the hollow of her throat.

His kisses trailed upward until, against her ear, she heard him whisper, "Lindsey, please say you'll marry me."

A yes, mingled with doubts of confusion warred in her mind. "Right now, Keaton, there's nothing I'd rather do. But there're so many reasons I shouldn't."

"Oh, yeah?" his voice held a confident air. His gaze found hers. "Name two."

"Keaton . . ."

"I am most definitely not a reason we shouldn't. Besides we don't have time for your stalling."

Lindsey furrowed her brow. She thought they still had a few weeks left before she had to decide.

"Sunday School starts in half an hour."

Lindsey laughed and pushed against his chest as she moved back inside. Something scampered across her foot. She screamed and jumped onto the bed as a three inch lizard, missing a tail, ran the opposite direction. Keaton lunged for the reptile as the doorway filled with excited children.

"Did you catch 'im?" Josh slid on his knees over to Keaton.

With a broad grin, he brought his fist forward for all to see. Between his thumb and the bend of his forefinger peeked a lizard's head.

***

Lindsey shifted in the upholstered pew. Though she was usually comfortable, today's sermon seemed written specifically for her. She almost wished she'd accepted Keaton's offer and attended church with him.

Her eyes glanced upward. *Sorry, God. I know we can't grow without a little discomfort.*

Though at first it seemed odd the pastor would be talking about the virgin birth in the middle of August, Lindsey knew it had to be the work of the Spirit.

The pastor's gentle voice helped her relax. "An angel told Mary not to be afraid, God would be with her and protect her. Mary had to accept this news. She had to decide to surrender."

He looked across the congregation. "Are some of you struggling with your fate? Perhaps you've prayed for God to do big things in your life, but fear is keeping you from accepting His answer."

Beads of perspiration formed along Lindsey's hairline. *God, if marrying Keaton is my fate, how can I tell my church? I'm not strong, I'm not courageous . . . I'm just me.*

Like Aaron being sent to help Moses, Sharon, sitting at the end of Lindsey's pew, scooted to her side. She placed a warm hand over Lindsey's white-knuckled fist and whispered a prayer for her ears alone. "Your Word tells us we can do all things through You because You strengthen us. Give her courage, Lord, to carry out what you've asked of her."

The pastor drew the sermon to a close and Lindsey knew it was now or never. On shaky knees, she stood, keeping Sharon's hand clasped tight in her own. Before she could utter a word, her bottom lip quivered and tears began to fall, stinging her eyes with their salt. She sniffed several times and tried to speak. A glance across the room showed others, seated in the pews, begin to cry with her. Their love made what she had to tell them that much harder. She didn't want to lose their support.

Through a tear-thickened voice, she relayed the situation Mike had created. Quick to defend Keaton's honor, amid gasps of disbelief, she wanted them to understand he wasn't to blame and had never pressured her. At least not in a negative way.

More like a loving, pleading way.

Why did she want to defend him so readily?

Without time for further thought, Mr. Sanders stood. "I can give you money from the sale of a couple cows."

The couple in front of her turned around. "We have an extra car you can have."

"We have a big empty basement." Sharon patted her hand. "Your family would be welcome to stay with us."

Lindsey's mouth dropped open. She had dreaded their response would match her in-laws. Such generosity had never been expected. How wrong she'd been to compare them. New tears slipped from her eyes as she realized comparisons rarely worked with people.

***

Lindsey drove to Keaton's farm in a confused state of mind. What did God expect her to do? She'd almost accepted that this marriage to Keaton was the right thing, what God wanted. Now, with the generosity of her church family, how was she to know what to do?

Elizabeth pierced her thoughts when she screamed, "Mouse!"

Lindsey glanced in the rearview mirror to see her children's frightened eyes. Her daughter had been serious. There was a mouse in her van. She hated things that scurried— and wondered briefly which was worse, a s lizard or a mouse?

Returning her attention back to the road, she looked for the nearest turn-off. The mouse scurried out from under her seat, ran between the brake and gas pedal then underneath the dash. Lindsey screamed and swerved at the same time. The van knifed to the side and off the road. She tried to correct the wheel but another bump jerked it from her hands. Out of control, the van careened past the ditch and smashed into a fence post.

The radiator hissed as the vehicle rocked to a halt. Lindsey peeled away her shaking hands from the steering wheel and turned to check on the children. One look at Clara was all it took for the little toddler to break into sobs. "Oh, Baby, it's all right."

She unhooked her seat-belt and removed Clara from the restraining seat. Holding her tight against her chest, she asked the other children, "Is everyone okay?"

Samantha nodded half-way to tears. The others looked at her with eyes open wide. Jack was the first to speak, "Hey, Mom, Clara made a sound."

He was right. Though it had been a cry, it was more noise than any of them had ever heard from the frightened child. "Clara, sweetie." Lindsey kissed her and held her closer still. A cry had never sounded so good.

Lindsey stepped from the van and looked back. She licked her swollen lip and tasted blood. She either bit her lip when they crashed or hit it against the steering wheel. "Come on out kids. It's too hot to stay in there." She checked each one for injury. "Thank God, we're not hurt."

Together, their little army walked to the front of the vehicle to survey the damage. Jack grabbed Josh's arm to stop him from touching the hood. "That steam is hot. You're gonna burn yourself."

"Thanks, Jack. You and Elizabeth will be my extra set of eyes. Everybody grab a buddy and the extra one, take my hand." She shifted Clara to her other arm. "Stay off the road, we're going for a walk."

Samantha ran to grab her hand. "Aunt Lin– I mean, Mama, is Daddy gonna be mad at you like Unc' Mike?"

Lindsey gave her hand a gentle squeeze. "No, honey. Keaton loves us, he won't be mad."

"Didn't Unc' Mike love us?"

Her question almost caused Lindsey to stumble. "Yes, he did. I meant Keaton loves your mama, so he won't be mad."

"Did Dad not love *you*, Mom?" Jack's sensitive, inquisitive nature didn't miss a beat.

Lindsey sighed. The van was wrecked and it was a hundred degrees, she didn't want to have to deal with trying to explain a man she'd never understood.

She opened her mouth to put the question off to a later time when a car slowed and pulled off to the side. Much to Lindsey's relief, Lucy bounded out of the driver's door.

Saved from walking and from talking!

By the time night allowed Lindsey to lay her head to rest, she willingly succumbed to the comfort of Keaton's bed. After today, she needed what pampering she could find. Since work had kept Keaton until the wee hours of the night on Saturday, he wasn't able to pick up her window. Which meant she still couldn't go home.

She struggled with what the right decision was. Marry Keaton or not, she still had Clayton to worry about.

***

Keaton grabbed the reports he'd finally finished and strode toward the office of the company president. Deadlines used to be the challenge he looked forward to, but lately, his passion for his job had all but expired. He and Denton were both favored for Mike's position. Was it wrong to hope it was rewarded to Denton?

He rapped on the door and was signaled in. Mr. Stone stood from behind his desk. "Keaton, come on in and take a seat." One of the reasons Keaton worked so hard was because of this man. Mr. Stone's respect for his workers had earned him an outstanding reputation. The gifted man had a way of encouraging everyone to reach higher. Keaton didn't like the idea of disappointing him and had even found himself emulating him in how he related to other people.

The company president accepted the files and set them aside on the desk as Keaton took his seat. Keaton glanced at the folders that had bound him to his desk all morning and back toward the man tapping his fingers. "Sir, don't you want to go over the report?"

A determined gaze pinned Keaton to his seat. But he wasn't one to squirm, he had nothing to hide. Still, the unusual look in Mr. Stone's eyes left him baffled.

"Mr. Durham, I have to confess, you're the one I want for Mike's job. Denton's a good man, and fully capable, but his drive can't mirror yours." He scratched his chin with the tip of his finger. "But I confess, recently I've grown concerned. It seems you've been distracted here of late and I'd like to know if that distraction has been resolved."

Keaton rubbed his hand over the back of his neck. His distraction with Lindsey must've shown up at work, but he didn't know how. Mr. Stone's voice interrupted his thoughts. "I was told you left recently, in the middle of the day, due to a call. Was this a family emergency?"

"Sort of." It was a lousy answer, but all he had to give.

His boss seemed to stare through him for a moment before relaxing back in his chair. "You're of good character, son. But you know you're needed here. You don't have the family that Denton has. I could use your devotion to this job. So wrap up any lose ends you have and jump back in the game. There's a hefty salary waiting for you."

Once the meeting was dismissed, Keaton took advantage of an outside job. It didn't matter that it was clean-up, he needed the space to clear his head. He couldn't be swayed by salary. He'd never needed much to live on. But Mr. Stone's mention of devotion continued to bother him.

Like a picture book unfolding, it became clear. Mike had always been on call. Work had become his home–his devotion. Keaton struggled with whether or not he could give that much.

Unlike Keaton, Denton had payments to meet; a house, a couple of cars, credit card debt. His family could use the extra money. Before Lindsey, Keaton would probably have strived to do whatever his boss had asked. The only thing he'd had waiting for him at the end of the day were cattle.

Now, everything had changed.

" . . . *There's a hefty salary waiting for you.*" It had never mattered to Keaton what he made. He led a simple life and only had to provide for himself.

But if he won Lindsey's hand, he'd have to provide for a family as well. Could he do that on his salary?

Lindsey drove a used van, her kids wore hand-me-downs. Though his current salary wouldn't provide worldly fineries, it would still provide well for them. It helped that Lindsey and the kids weren't used to living in expense.

What did Mike do with all his money? The question wasn't one he would have given thought to under different circumstances. But now, the question deserved an answer. The home he'd bought was aged and in need of repair. His family didn't live in excess of anything.

Hunting trips.

Mike would take expensive hunting vacations, the kind average people didn't take. Pictures of his escapades were still pasted at his desk.

"Your hunting dog."

Lindsey's disgust with his dog suddenly became clear. Mike had never included his family in his vacations. Did Lindsey fear he would do the same? Keaton almost laughed out loud. Samson was more like someone's pampered poodle than a hunter. He'd have to let Lindsey know. A beef farmer didn't have need for hunting, and he was too soft to do it for sport.

Keaton finished the clean-up and marched back to Mr. Stone's office. It was time to set things right.

***

"Samantha! We don't swing on cabinet doors." Lindsey pulled her niece to a kitchen chair. "Chairs are for sitting. Now what would you do if that had broken? You'd have had to tell Keaton."

"You mean, Daddy."

Lindsey sighed and rubbed her forehead. Thoughts of the church congregation had bombarded her all day. Even with their offers, peace still eluded her. Independence would still be out of reach as she'd have to move in with someone. Not all their offered money put together could buy her home or support her and the children.

Lucy called from the front porch. "Hey, crazy woman-behind-a-wheel, are you home?"

Lindsey sighed with relief. Yesterday she'd upset Lucy by sharing about the church offers. She was glad to hear the notes of happiness had returned to her voice. Lindsey smiled and met Samantha's excited eyes. She touched the tip of her nose. "Beat you to the door!"

Samantha squealed as she slid from the chair and wiggled past Lindsey. She ran into Lucy's open arms, proud of her first place accomplishment. "I beat Mama."

"Mama, is it?" Lucy's curious glance moved from the exuberant child to Lindsey.

"Uh, huh. And Keaton my daddy."

Lucy's smile turned smug. "I'm glad to hear it. You know what that makes me?" At the child's shake of her head, she added, "Your aunt."

Moments later, Lindsey and Lucy sat on the porch steps with ice tea and watched the children play. "I never told them I was marrying Keaton. They've just teamed up against me."

Lucy interrupted a quarrel between two of the children. "Josh, if you tagged her then you've got stretchy arms. I think you need to try again." She turned her attention back to Lindsey. "What are you not saying?"

"Why couldn't Mike have given me six months? At least people might half-way understand that."

"So that's what this is all about– You don't want to marry my brother because of what others think?"

"It's more than that." Lindsey worried her bottom lip with her fingers. "Who am I, Lucy? I was Mike's wife. I wasn't allowed an opinion. Even if I was brave enough to voice one, it was always wrong or stupid. Now that I'm free I'd like to find out who I am. What my likes and dislikes are. How *I* perceive what's going on in the world, not what someone *tells* me what to think."

"And you think *Keaton* would *tell* you what to think?"

Lindsey ran a hand through her hair. "No. He wouldn't. But I already know enough about myself, I'd want to agree with him just to please him."

"And why do you want to please him—out of fear?"

Lindsey peered closer at her friend. "No! There's nothing to be afraid of with Keaton."

"Then ask yourself why you'd want to please him. And when you get that figured out, consider where you'll be without him." Lucy set her jaw and shook her head with frustration. "Even if your church gets you out of the jam Mike created, do you want someone else holding my brother's heart? One, two, three years down the line? He's too special for someone not to snatch him up, you know."

Lucy didn't wait for an answer and stood to leave. "I almost forgot, here." She held out a folded piece of paper. "These are notes from the sermon I heard yesterday. I think you should read them. I've gotta go."

Lindsey's eyes stung as she watched Lucy say good-bye to the children and walk across the road to her mother's cabin. She'd upset her again.

The screen door opened behind Lindsey and out walked Jack. "When are you going to marry Keaton?"

Lindsey sighed and blinked rapidly to dry her eyes. "Why are you in a hurry to replace your dad?" Guilt churned her stomach. Her voice had sounded stern. She shouldn't have taken her frustration out on her son.

She expected him to get mad and walk away. Instead, Jack shoved his thumbs in his pockets and looked at the floor of the porch. He cocked his head to the side and glanced at her—an exact mimic of Keaton. "Dad was never around much, Mom. He never took us on vacation, and he was never happy with anything you did. Keaton likes you and he likes us kids."

He took a step toward the door. "I've already talked to everyone else. We all want you to be happy, Mom, and we want Keaton to be our dad."

The screen door banged shut as her son reentered the house leaving Lindsey to sit in stunned silence.

Chapter Thirteen

Keaton walked to the parking lot twenty minutes past his shift. Though he'd stayed late to finish a machine, knowing he wouldn't constantly be on call made him feel like a new man.

He slowed his pace as he approached the back of the lot. The driver's side door of his Bronco hung slightly ajar. The nice thing about driving an aged vehicle, only the driver knew all its quirks. For the door to latch, it had to be lifted while being shut. Someone had opened it while he was working. He glanced around.

Perhaps one of the guys pulled a joke. Just last week a mechanic had found a racoon in the back of his truck. That had earned a lot of laughs.

A prickly sensation on the back of his neck warned him otherwise. Swinging the door wide, he did a quick inventory of the interior. Nothing out of place.

He walked to the front and opened the hood. The battery cables and spark plug wires were still connected. Nothing appeared tampered with. He closed the hood and got behind the wheel. Maybe he hadn't shut the door this morning.

The drive home helped shake the feeling that he'd missed something. With the windows down, the hot August air made him long for the river. He hoped Lindsey and the kids were enjoying the creek that ran by the house. A small bridge, left from his childhood, still reached between the banks where he and Lucy had spent most of their summers playing.

An earlier comment of hers captured his thoughts. She'd said Lindsey wanted a fairy-tale. He already thought of her as his princess, perhaps it was time to convince her. Maybe he could weave it into their wedding.

He pulled into his driveway. Though it had been an exhausting day, he still had a job, and better, now he'd have time for a family. He met Lindsey at the door. Her broad smile kindled a fire inside him. The closer he drew, the hotter it burned.

He stopped just out of reach, knowing if he came any closer he'd pull her into his arms. Her eyes danced. She had to know what he was feeling.

She pinched her bottom lip between her teeth. "So this is what it would be like?"

Keaton couldn't contain himself, he narrowed the distance. "You mean if we were married?"

She gave a small nod. Keaton shook his head and closed the space between them. The scent of her shampoo heightened his senses. Sliding an arm behind her neck, he leaned her back. "Nope. *This* is what it would be like."

Just as his lips neared hers, Elizabeth ran to the door. "Dad's home! Eww, and he's kissing Mom."

Moments later, with a sandwich in their hands for dinner, Keaton and Lindsey pulled away in his Bronco to fix the window at her house while it was yet light. Lindsey's eyes seemed to probe through him. "You seem extra happy about something. How about a nickel for your thoughts?"

A laugh rumbled from his chest. "Are you that desperate? People used to only offer a penny."

"Did I get it wrong again?" A shamed smile graced her face.

"Never." Keaton reached for her hand. "You always get it right, because you always make me smile."

A glow emanated from Lindsey. It took so little to please her. Keaton wanted to find even more ways to do so. Every little step toward rebuilding her confidence was a step toward more smiles. More happiness.

Keaton faked a big sigh. "Well, if you must know . . ." He watched the anticipation build across her features. "I turned down a really big raise today."

Her mouth twitched as if unsure whether it was allowable to smile or not. But her eyes couldn't hold back their excitement. With obvious effort at control, she asked, "What do you mean?"

"I mean, from here on out, I'm just you're regular mechanic with regular hours. I refused the position of manager so I could spend more time with a particular family."

Giant tears pooled in Lindsey's eyes. Her nose turned a soft shade of pink followed by a sniff. "You did that for us?"

Keaton pulled over to the side of the road and stepped on the brake. He turned toward Lindsey and ran a finger under her eye to catch a tear. "It was an easy decision. Think you can handle having me around that much?"

Lindsey threw her arms around him in a tight embrace. "Yes." As she slowly pulled away, she whispered, "Thank you, Keaton. You make me so happy."

Keaton swallowed the urge to ask her to marry him, yet again. He was making progress. Patience would win more points than pushing. He pulled back onto the county road and shifted gears as they drove down a hill. The Bronco bounced along the gravel, sending his phone sliding from its precarious perch near the gearshift and to the floor. Lindsey stretched to retrieve it but Keaton stopped her. "It's okay. We're almost there." He noted her furrowed brow. "What?"

She glanced at him and back to the floorboard. "Do you smoke?"

"No, you know that." Keaton pulled up to her house and shut off the engine. With one more glance in her direction he stepped out and bent to grab his phone. Then he saw the reason for her question. What looked like a used, short cigarette now lay beside his dropped phone. Keaton picked it up and held it out for Lindsey to see.

"That's not a cigarette."

"I was afraid of that." He peered under his seat and blew out a sigh. Grabbing a shop towel from the back, he removed another one. "Clayton."

He walked Lindsey to the door with every nerve tensed. When had Clayton planted the drugs in his vehicle? And what good would framing him do? He unlocked the door and crossed inside first. Once assured everything else was as it should be, he stepped aside and motioned for Lindsey. "I'll be back after I bag the evidence."

Again, he used the shop towel to avoid touching the marijuana joints. Though his prints would probably show on the one he first handled, at least it wouldn't on both. He folded the bag into his shirt pocket and clasped the button to keep from losing them. His eyes caught sight of the hand-held recorder he carried with him to meetings. Grabbing it, he slid it in his other pocket and returned to the house.

"I'm sorry you're in this mess, Keaton." Lindsey ran a hand through her long auburn hair and tossed it over one shoulder. She looked lost standing in the middle of her living room staring at nothing. Keaton pulled her to him and rubbed his cheek against her hair.

"Don't. You know I'm right where I want to be." He reached for her left hand and raked his thumb over her empty ring finger. "Well . . . almost."

A slow smile graced her mouth. She leaned forward and kissed him with a deliberate passion that sent his heart racing. Encouraged, he drew her closer. The feel of her beneath his hands set his blood to pumping. She unknowingly tempted him to the outer limits. He'd waited so long for moments like this he never wanted it to end. But it had to. They were alone and the thoughts that tempted his mind would have to wait. At least for a couple more weeks.

The phone rang, cutting through the silence of the empty house. Lindsey sighed and moved away. She tried to hide her disappointment over the interruption with a lift of her shoulder, but Keaton saw through it. He was winning her over–finally.

He motioned with his hand and reached into his pocket. "Wait. I'll grab the other phone." Not waiting to explain, he pushed record and counted to three with his fingers before they each picked up a receiver.

"Hello." Lindsey's voice sounded timid.

"You're not very smart are you, girly?" Clayton's voice rasped. Anger welled inside Keaton as he clinched the phone tighter.

"You never should've called the cops. Now it's gonna cost you." He paused, Lindsey didn't reply. "Did you know the law still gives me full rights as a dad? Guardianship only means you can take care of a kid."

"Stop it, Clayton."

His laugh sounded harsh. "Oh no, little one, I've just started."

Lindsey slid down the wall as the phone went dead. Keaton knelt by her side and rubbed his hand over her arm. "I have him on tape. We have the paraphilia he left in the Bronco. He'll never get custody of the girls."

Lindsey gave a feeble nod of her head and stared at the floor. A knock on the front door drew him to his feet. Fist clenched, he was ready to hurt Clayton.

But it wasn't a man.

He opened the door with Lindsey by his side. She was the first to speak. "May we help you?"

"I hope so. I've tried to contact you all weekend but no one was home." She held out her hand. "I'm Gwenna Roberts from DFS, Division of Family Services. May I come in?"

Lindsey visibly paled as she stumbled backward. Keaton caught her elbow and tried for a show of normalcy but inside his mind reeled. Had Clayton gone through the trouble of setting them up?

"Let's have a seat, shall we?" Ms. Roberts motioned to the table. "I think we'll be comfortable for the beginning of our meeting right here. Where are the children?"

Lindsey spoke, barely above a whisper. "They're staying at a friend's house while we fix the window."

Ms. Roberts looked toward the window then down at the floor as her feet crunched on top of missed pieces of broken glass. Lindsey pulled at her lip, "I tried to sweep it all up but we left in a hurry and I haven't been back."

An eyebrow raised on the social worker's face. "Do you mind filling me in?"

Lindsey wrapped her arms around her stomach. "Why are you here?"

"There's been a report filed. I'm only here to do my job, Lindsey. May I call you that?"

She muttered under her breath, "Time will tell."

Once seated, Ms. Roberts opened her folder and readied her pen. Lindsey explained the reason for the broken window as the social worker filled in her report. "And you say this man is the biological father of one of your nieces' and possibly both of them?"

"Unfortunately, yes." Lindsey swiped a hand over her forehead and through her hair. She was tiring and there was nothing Keaton could do. He longed to draw her to his side and let her lean against him drawing from his strength. But whatever act of affection he showed would go directly in Ms. Roberts' report.

The woman tapped her pen on top of the paper. "You said your husband passed away recently. Are his effects still in the house?"

"Yes, but why does that matter?"

"I need to take a look around, and knowing his things are still in place helps you. It shows you aren't in a hurry to hide something." Ms. Roberts rose and started toward the hall. "First I need to check your plumbing, to verify you have running water."

Keaton met Lindsey's wide eyes. The social worker's actions were bewildering. And if Lindsey's shocked look was any indication, she felt the same. They followed her to the kitchen and found her opening cabinet doors and the refrigerator, jotting down notes in her folder.

She turned toward them. "I take it this is your first visit from DFS. Don't worry, this is common procedure. I have to verify the children aren't being deprived of food."

Lindsey closed a door on the cabinet. "Then I'm afraid I'll have points against me. My late husband never allowed for extra spending."

"Well, now that he's passed, you can change things."

Keaton watched Lindsey work at controlling her facial expression. She couldn't change anything, Mike was still in control, but to allow Ms. Roberts that information would only lead to further questioning.

The evening wore on with Lindsey being drilled with question after question while Keaton replaced the window and responded when needed. He almost thought she believed the truth until her last question. "May I see your closets?"

Keaton couldn't have kept his mouth closed with a clamp. "What–why?"

"This isn't your house, Mr. Durham, so please don't interfere. Besides, you don't want to know the stories I could tell to support this part of the process. You'd be shocked at what we find."

Keaton couldn't believe what she was implying. Did people actually hide their children in closets? For what cause, unless it was to conceal their abusive behavior.

The drive home was filled with a restless void. Lindsey sat in the passenger seat, her knees drawn to her like a ball. Fear of what thoughts filled her mind warned him not to ask. He didn't listen. "What are you thinking?"

She sighed and rested her head against the seat. "Of what the sunset reminds me of."

Keaton looked out her window. The sun sat low over a hay field giving it the illusion of a blaze of fire.

"Lauren and I were running home from the creek." The sound of the engine made her soft voice hard to hear. "We'd spent all afternoon there. She was twelve, I was ten. As we ran through a field like that one, we pretended the earth was at its end. That the sun had fallen from the sky."

Silence encased them. Keaton reached for her hand and she clasped it tight. "The earth may not have ended that night, but what was left of my childhood did. We stopped at the fence separating the field from our house to see whose car was there." Her hand became rigid inside his palm. "It was Uncle Gary's. He wasn't really our uncle— he just made us call him that. I never liked him, but my sister did. He treated her . . . special."

She batted her eyes but a tear still fell. "That night, my parents said she was old enough to stay for the party. I begged her not to," her voice cracked, "but she wouldn't listen."

Keaton struggled to breath. They'd purposefully led their child into drugs. The thought was too disturbing to wrap his head around. He wrung the steering wheel with his hand. God clearly stated what would come to those who mistreated His children. His word said it'd be better for a millstone to be tied around their neck and they be drowned in the sea than the fate that awaited them. Thank God for His justice.

Lindsey withdrew into an eerie silence. Keaton didn't ask her to continue. He didn't want to imagine. His heart tore from her pain. Not only had she endured such a childhood, now after trying so hard to be the opposite of the example set by her parents, she was being accused of equal failure. Anger boiled inside him.

Like their conversation, their drive came to an end. Lindsey clung to Keaton in the doorway of his home as he said good-night. She whimpered out loud, "I can't lose my children, Keaton. Pray, pray I don't lose them."

"Since that woman came to the house, I haven't stopped." Not even married, and they already faced more trouble than some marriages bear in a life-time.

He walked across the road, his mind too numb to think. The same reoccurring prayer that he'd whispered all night again ran through his mind. *God, keep Lindsey's family together. And keep them with me.* He ran a hand over his face and reached for his folks' door. It opened from inside and Lucy stepped out.

Despite the strain of the evening, Keaton mustered a weary smile. "Hey, Sis."

"We need to talk." The fact that she skipped pleasantries made his senses come alert. Had Clayton's treachery reached the farm?

He didn't have to ask. Evidently whatever was wrong had weighed on Lucy's heart long enough, she wasn't about to keep it to herself a moment longer. "Lindsey's church has bought her a way out."

Chapter Fourteen

Like a china plate dropped on the floor, Keaton's hope shattered. He didn't know Lindsey still wanted a way out. He shook his head. He needed more information.

"Lindsey told the congregation about what Mike did. That she had to marry you. And they started offering her money, cars, houses, the works." She placed a hand on his shoulder. "You needed to know. I love you, Keaton. I don't want you hurt."

His throat constricted with a failed attempt to swallow. It didn't add up. Lindsey had kissed him tonight, last night . . . like she was finally falling in love. Why would she accept their offers? And where did they come up with the money? Where was God in all of this?

"I have to get home." She stalled in front of him. "I want you two together, Keaton. I didn't want to tell you, but you had to know."

He stared at her, not moving. Deaf ears not wanting to accept what he'd heard. "I'm going for a walk."

Crickets and whippoorwills smothered the crunch of gravel under foot as he crossed the road.

He hadn't planned on where to walk, but his course naturally led him closer to Lindsey.

She must've confided in Lucy on Sunday. Why not with him, unless she hadn't wanted to accept their offer? He knew she wasn't one to use him simply to stay in his house. Lindsey was too pure for actions like that. So different from those who'd raised her.

Samson lumbered over and stuck his cold, wet nose in Keaton's palm then rubbed his bony head against his leg. Together, they walked the shadowed perimeter as he'd done the night before. A low, cloud cover hid the stars and brought a familiar scent of rain in the air. Keaton inhaled deeply, searching for a way to relax. It didn't help.

He stared at the back of his farmhouse. The light upstairs switched off. As he imagined the children nestled in their beds, he could almost hear their peaceful breathing. He and Lindsey could tuck them in together, lead them in bedtime prayers. That is, if she gave him a chance. But if she didn't . . .

Slowly, in mocking deliberateness, the vision of each child vanished from their beds, one by one. Rumpled covers and scattered toys would serve as a reminder of his loss. A haunting emptiness constricted his chest. He couldn't imagine life without them. A life without their mother.

"God, don't take them away. Help her see what we could have." He swiped a hand over his face then paused.

Lindsey's voice floated to him on the breeze. Who was she talking to? Keaton crept closer and saw her shadowed form leaning on the porch railing outside his bedroom. Her head was bowed in prayer.

". . . I've fallen in love. If it's wrong to marry Keaton, show me, Lord. Otherwise, please bless us . . ."

Air rushed back into Keaton's lungs. He hadn't meant to overhear Lindsey's prayer. But he had. Thank God, he had.

**

Late the next afternoon, Lindsey watched Ms. Roberts pull into Keaton's driveway. Ann stood by her side twirling a strand of hair. "Keep praying, Lindsey. God's in control."

Ann had taken such a liking to Lindsey's family, that despite her words of confidence, Lindsey knew they battled the same weight of worry. She squeezed her hand for a quick sharing of strength before opening the door.

Ms. Roberts strode inside with a friendly nature. She smiled warmly and gave a quick glance at the interior of the front room before greeting Lindsey, then Ann. "Hello, I remember you from the food pantry. You help out on Wednesdays, right?"

Lindsey breathed a sigh of relief. A positive, common ground. *Thank you, God.*

She hoped the children remembered what they'd been told. "Do not refer to Keaton as your daddy. Ms. Roberts wants to know about your real daddy. If she asks about Keaton, call him by his name." She didn't want to mislead the social worker, but she definitely didn't want to give her added reason to doubt her ability to make sound decisions. The probability of her understanding her current predicament wasn't something Lindsey was willing to risk.

After the initial meeting of the children, Ms. Roberts turned to Lindsey. "Your children are certainly delightful, Lindsey. You must be proud."

"I am, thank you."

"This meeting has gone very well. I really don't see any reason that would require we meet again. Sometimes calls are put through out of a misunderstanding and I believe that's all that happened here."

Lindsey exhaled, releasing the tension in her shoulders. She closed the door behind Ms. Roberts and leaned against it, her energy sapped. Ann mirrored her as she slid onto the cushion of Keaton's couch.

"Thank you for being here, Ann. I don't think I could've coped without you."

Ann's eyes became moist. "It's I who should thank you. You and your children have brought such a blessing to our farm." She paused as Clara climbed into her lap. "I hope you're planning on staying."

If there was a question behind her statement, she didn't push for an answer. Lindsey appreciated her for that, but knew she needed to put Ann's heart at ease. "I've fallen in love with your son, Ann." The words tumbled from her mouth.

She had meant to explain how she'd felt about Mike's controlling plan and build up to her feelings for Keaton, but her heart had jumped ahead of her.

A genuine smile stretched across Ann's face, lighting her features with a happy glow. She swallowed and hugged Clara, her soon-to-be *granddaughter*, tight against her.

***

The following afternoon, Lindsey peered inside Keaton's refrigerator. What could she put together for lunch? Although he'd brought home some staples, he really knew nothing about grocery shopping for a family of eight. She longed to run errands but since driving her van into a fence post, that option would have to wait.

Elizabeth entered from outside. Sweat dampened the hair around her face and her cheeks were red from the exertion of play. She stood beside her mom. "Let's go grocery shopping."

Lindsey smiled and draped an arm over her slender shoulders. "Great idea, but I don't have any wheels."

"Can't Ann take us?"

"No. She's helping at the food pantry today." She smiled at the irony.

Samson bayed as someone pulled into their driveway. Lindsey and Elizabeth hurried outside to see who it was and make sure the children were safe out of the way.

Lindsey smiled and waved as Carol and Harold, members of her church, pulled into Keaton's driveway in two different vehicles. She walked to greet them with her rag-tag bundle of kids. Dirt smeared their sweat-dampened clothing. They needed baths and clean clothes, but she hadn't had the heart to stop their play. They were having so much fun being on the farm.

The children offered hugs which were well received despite their playful state of attire. Lindsey glanced between the vehicles and asked with growing curiosity, "Not that I'm not thrilled to see you, but what are you two doing out here?"

Harold grinned and looked at his wife and back to Lindsey. "We thought you might need an extra set of wheels until yours are fixed."

Lindsey gasped. Word traveled quickly. "Oh no, I couldn't.'"

Carol stepped forward and pushed her van keys into Lindsey's palm. "Yes, you can. We know your van will be in the shop for the rest of the week and thought you might need a way to get around. It's big enough to seat everyone."

"Take it, Mom. Yay, we get to go to town!" Elizabeth's comment made it hard to refuse.

Lindsey fought the tremor in her lip. Their generous hearts overwhelmed her. "Thank you. I do need to buy groceries. And the kids enjoy going with me. Can I bring it back to you on Sunday? I should have my van by then. Keaton could drive one of the vehicles and everyone at church could meet him."

Harold placed a hand on his wife's shoulder. "That would be a good idea. I'd like to meet the man you think so highly of."

Lindsey furrowed her brow. "What do you mean? I haven't spoken of him before Sunday."

Carol smile and patted her hand. "But what you did say spoke volumes."

Lindsey dropped her gaze to the gravel at her feet. How could she be so transparent and before she'd even understood her own feelings? She wished the earth would swallow her whole. They had known Mike.

Carol covered her hand with her own. "Lindsey, I saw through Mike. I know enough of what your life was like, I would never think awful of you. If this is your chance at happiness—at love, then take it."

Speechless, Lindsey accepted Carol's embrace then watched them leave in the other vehicle. The keys to their van were still clutched in her hand. Carol had seen through Mike. Perhaps others had seen past his façade.

Relief coursed through her. Now she could love Keaton without guilt. The sound of a door slam stole her attention. The kids were inside the van, smiles plastered their faces. Lindsey laughed at their excitement over a different vehicle. Children were so easy to please. Although they were all sweaty and their clothes dirty from play, she didn't have the heart to tell them no. They could take baths after town.

She installed their car-seats and strapped everyone in. The van wasn't very different from hers, but she still paid careful attention. She couldn't risk damaging a vehicle that didn't belong to her.

The drive into town offered time for her thoughts. She couldn't get past Carol's comment. Mike had always played a perfect front in public, making a big deal of wanting her opinion, or cupping her hand in his arm when they walked out the door. His public display embarrassed her. The attention was fake, and she hadn't wanted to play along. But anytime she'd try to withdraw or pretend not to notice, his eyes would narrow, threatening a verbal lashing at home, followed by his form of punishment, ignoring her presence and overly doting on the children. It always caused bedlam in the household.

Her hands hurt from the tight grip she held on the wheel. Thoughts of Mike's controlling behavior still stressed her. She had to work past this. Lucy had confided she'd taken a year of counseling after the death of her husband, though her family didn't know. She'd shared the steps to recovery after living under emotional abuse. Lindsey had paid careful attention. She'd already mastered the first step, being honest with her abuse. The second step took a lot more effort, forgiving the abuser.

While she worked on forgiveness, she also had to surrender her coping mechanisms. For so long, she'd blocked others from her life, accepting Mike's words as truth, that no one would like her because she was so incompetent, and she always lied.

She knew she didn't lie. That was just his way of breaking down her self-confidence, causing her to doubt any decision she tried to make. She now had to accept the intelligence God gave her and that He created her worthy of friendship as well as love. Whether Keaton realized what he was doing or not, he helped build her up every day. Asking for her opinion in everything and complimenting her decisions.

He showed her love.

"Mama, can we get a sucker at the bank?" Josh was thinking ahead.

"I want a blue one."

"I want bubble-gum!"

Lindsey interrupted them. "You'll have to take what you get. Now quiet down, we're almost there."

Moments later, Lindsey pulled away from the bank with an eerie feeling of being watched. She glanced down the street. Everything appeared normal. Cars stopped at the intersection, a faded red pickup sat down the block and she recognized a couple of men from church sitting outside the barber shop talking "shop."

She attributed the feeling to being overly paranoid and continued her errands.

The grocery store was their only other stop.

Half-way through the store, Lindsey had to count heads again. "Someone's missing. Jack, see if Samantha's still on the other aisle. Kids, you have to stay with me."

Jack returned with his cousin and they resumed shopping. Twenty minutes later, Lindsey had everyone and their groceries loaded and couldn't wait to be home. The children were all tired, which resulted in arguments and whining. At the last stop-light she threw the car in park and turned around in her seat. Her patience was spent.

"What is all the fighting for?"

Bradley pointed a stubby finger. "Sissy, not share her candy."

"Nobody has candy—" Her words were cut off by Samantha's continuous laughter. "Samantha, what's in your mouth?"

It was clear she was sucking on something and their suckers had been finished long ago. A horn honked behind her, signally the change of the red light. Stress tightened the muscles in her shoulders. "Samantha, spit it out. What do you have?"

Lindsey reached around to squeeze her niece's cheeks but dropped her hand in shock. In between her fit of giggles, Samantha opened red rimmed, puffy eyes. Panic surged through Lindsey as she fumbled with the release button of her belt.

The car honked again, followed by another. Lindsey clamored to the bench seat and forced Samantha's mouth open. She threw the candy on the floor and grabbed her in her arms.

The results of a high were all too familiar.

Chapter Fifteen

Lindsey slid into a waiting room chair with Clara pressed against her. The shaking of her knee caps had forced her to stop pacing. Watching Samantha being rolled away on the gurney was more than she could take. Her throat constricted as though she'd swallowed a ball that was stuck halfway down. Her children sat unusually quiet, their eyes large with fear. No one spoke, but she was sure they shared the same fears. Would Samantha be okay?

She was amazed they'd arrived at the hospital without incident. She'd driven fanatically through town, weaving between cars, running stoplights. The whole time her mind reeling over facts she didn't want to face.

Like a nightmare come alive, her worst fear had materialized. Her daily prayer included her children would always say no to drugs. Never would she have imagined any of them would consume it accidentally. Had someone handed the candy to her niece, or did she find it on the floor? To add to her worries, the possibility of an allergic reaction taunted her mind. If Samantha had an allergy to whatever drug was used to lace the candy it could easily lead to heart problems. Or worse . . .

Her lip quivered uncontrollably as her entire body trembled. She had to get control. From the corner of her eye, she saw Jack reach for his siblings' hands. With his head bowed, he prayed, "God, please help Samantha get well and help Mama not be so scared. Amen."

She blinked against an onslaught of tears. Tragedy had turned her baby into a man. She pulled her shoulders back and drew in a deep breath, borrowing strength from his prayer.

The automatic doors opened admitting a blast of hot air followed by a stern-faced woman and two policemen. The click of her heels sounded like a death toll. They were headed straight toward Lindsey. Clara squirmed in her arms and whimpered as a uniformed officer approached.

"Lindsey Buchannan? I'm Officer Cooper. We've sent the candy to the lab but it would help if you could tell us what happened."

Lindsey slumped further into the chair. It would help them, if only she knew. "We were at the grocery store." She tried to control the tremor in her voice. "I turned to count heads and Samantha was missing. Jack found her on the last aisle we'd been on. She acted fine. We finished up and were on our way. But in the van she was laughing . . . it was out of place. She looked wrong. She, she," Lindsey choked back a sob. "I grabbed her and opened her mouth to remove the candy."

"Did you notice anyone paying extra attention to the children?"

"No. Nothing like that." She sniffed. "The children were getting tired, and I was ready to go home."

"If you think of anything else, even if it might seem like nothing, I want to be informed."

The officer stepped aside as the woman who'd entered with him moved closer. The policeman must have realized he'd gotten all the information he could and left them to talk.

"I'm Noel Adams, with DFS. I know you're going through a lot right now, but I have to ask you some questions." She gave a cursory glance toward the children and paused. Lindsey knew their soiled clothing had captured her attention.

"Where's Ms. Roberts?" Her voice wobbled but at least she'd been able to form a question.

"Ms. Roberts has appointments lined up for the rest of the day. But not to worry, I've been in contact with her." Her voice had softened, she had a heart. Her eyes filled with concern as she pulled over a chair.

"I understand you've had trouble with a family member. The police are doing all they can." She paused with apparent hesitation, and continued. "I still have to ask you some questions."

Lindsey shuddered as she exhaled and tried to regain enough strength to get through. Where was Keaton? She'd asked the hospital staff to call him. She needed his support, his strength.

***

Keaton rushed through the emergency doors, unsure of what he'd find. He turned to the waiting room and saw Lindsey surrounded by children and a woman in a suit, poised with a pen and clipboard; she all but screamed *social worker*. He stepped toward Lindsey, but a small flick of her hand stopped him. The children ran to his side, but it was Lindsey who held his rapt attention. Her pallor had lost its color and brown patches settled below her eyes.

Keaton picked up Clara in answer to her pleading arms while he greeted the other children. Their young voices rose in anxious chatter as they fought to relay their own versions of what had happened. Keaton glanced back at Lindsey and swallowed against his building frustration. She needed his support. The children began to argue as to whose story was right when Keaton could take no more.

"Hush."

His single word encased in a stern tone brought complete silence. It was the first time he'd sounded anything but congenial. He strengthened himself against their sad faces. "What happened is very serious. I need to talk to your mother, but in order to do that, I want each of you to take a seat and be still."

"Yes, Keaton."

"Okay, Dad."

The mix of replies didn't go unnoticed. The suited woman arched an eyebrow and swiveled her clipboard in his direction. "Is he your boyfriend?"

Keaton disliked her for no other reason than the fear she toppled onto Lindsey's already growing list. And where was Ms. Roberts? He cleared his throat. "I'm a friend of the family. Mike and I worked together." He hoped his work relation with Mike would put an end to the reflective questions in her eyes.

Keaton directed the kids to the snack machine and bought them each a treat. He filled two coffees for Lindsey and himself. Regardless of the woman's over-bearing presence, he had to show his support. He guided the satisfied children back to the waiting room and sat in an empty seat beside Lindsey. She accepted the coffee with a grateful sigh.

He sipped his drink while silently willing the uninvited woman to leave. Lindsey leaned her head against his shoulder, as though too tired to be concerned with how the social worker would interpret her action.

"I'll leave you be for now. I'll talk to the staff then file my report. Ms. Roberts will see you tomorrow." The woman rose and disappeared down the hall.

Soon after, a nurse clad in white, entered the room. "Mrs. Buchannan, your niece is stable and doing well. You'll be able to see her in a few moments. We will of course keep her overnight for observation, but you're welcome to stay."

Tears of apparent relief coursed down Lindsey's cheeks. Keaton pulled her to him. With one hand gently cupped behind her head he rubbed his other hand over her back. "It's going to be okay. Thank You, Lord, it's going to be okay."

Lindsey's broken voice spoke against his shirt. "They sent the candy to the lab, and the police are having the candy from my house tested. I'm almost glad for the break-in, otherwise social services would be all over me."

"I thought she was."

"No. She had to ask the questions she did. It's her job."

A nurse reentered the room. "Miss, you can see your niece now."

Lindsey's worried eyes sought Keaton's. He pressed his lips to her forehead. He searched for what to say but until they were all home together, nothing would feel sure or safe. "I'll take the others home and I'll see you in the morning."

He switched keys with her and loaded the rest of the children into the van. Clara was unusually clingy and cried when he buckled her in.

Josh clapped. "Hey, Clara's making noise again!"

They made for an odd scene. A man with five children and one of them cheering the tears of another. Keaton tried to soothe the child's fears. "Mama and Samantha will be home tomorrow."

Clara pointed to the hospital. "Ma-ma."

Tears sprang to Keaton's eyes followed by the cheers of children. In the midst of trials, all it took was the smallest blessing to renew hope. Lindsey would be so proud to hear Clara's first word was all for her.

Keaton slowed his vehicle along the gravel road leading home. He glanced behind him, five sleepy heads bobbed up and down against their chests. Wrappers from their fast-food dinner littered their laps and the floor. His chest swelled with emotion. This is what it was like to be a father. He hadn't stopped to consider the role he'd so easily slipped into. Until now he'd felt more like a friend, but tonight, everything changed.

He pulled up to his parents' house. He needn't knock on the door, his mom and dad both stepped out, no doubt eager to hear about Samantha.

"She's going to be fine. Why don't you come over? You can help carry the kids in and we'll talk."

Keaton turned around then drove across the road to his house, thankful for his parents' help.

He would've never felt safe leaving the kids in the car as he carried one in at a time. Who knew where Clayton lurked now.

Jack was the last to be carried inside. Keaton scooped him in his arms while his parents gathered up the groceries. Sleepy eyes opened as he pulled the covers to the boy's chin. His small hand disturbed the sheet and grasped Keaton's arm. He mumbled, "Stay with us tonight, Dad."

"I will. I'll be downstairs if you need me." Keaton patted his shoulder then turned for the stairs.

Jack yawned. "I love you."

Keaton looked back. "I love you too, Son."

Son. The word slipped from his mouth and into his heart. Even before a vow could be spoken, he'd become a father to six children. His life was near full. Lindsey, as his wife, would complete it.

***

Lindsey stirred in the cot next to Samantha and listened to her breathing. Though the rise and fall of her chest kept a steady rhythm, the effort sounded more labored than normal. Sleep would help ease Lindsey's worries, but the thought of all that could have gone wrong kept jarring her awake every time she would start to doze.

She swung her feet to the floor and stared at the sleeping child. Her skin reflected the light of the moon, giving it a tint of blue. Lindsey shuddered.

God, forgive me when I fail. Know that I'll never purposefully hurt any of these children. Please don't take them from me. Not through death, and not through custody. No one could love them as much as I do.

She stood and crept to the window to draw the shade tighter. A star twinkled at her from millions of miles away. She pictured the earth as a small blue dot in the midst of a giant universe, yet God heard every uttered prayer.

Lindsey closed the curtain and stepped from the room. The chapel was down the hall not far from the entrance of the hospital. She needed a moment alone with God then perhaps she could sleep.

A diptych of stained glass windows stood out in the otherwise dull hallway. Lindsey opened the door to a small room with its only lighting coming from above the altar and the depiction of Jesus. Selecting the second pew from the front, she sat down, alone. The scene of Jesus weeping at the tomb of Lazarus struck her as an odd selection to choose for a hospital chapel. She stared at the precision of the artist's brush strokes, careful to the smallest detail such as the ends of Jesus' fingers and the folds in the fabric of his robe. Her eyes drew up to meet the eyes of her Creator. Her breath stalled.

Here was the Son of God, the Maker of all things, yet he experienced the same emotions as man. His friend had died. Mary and Martha, also his friends, were wrought with pain over the loss of their brother. Jesus' heart filled with compassion. So much compassion, that he wept.

Lindsey let her tears flow freely. No words were needed. Her Savior knew what she was going through, He had been there himself. She remained seated a few more minutes, willing the peace in the room to penetrate through her fears. She reached for a tissue as she stood to leave. Stepping into the hallway, she walked blindly toward her room as she fought to dry her eyes.

A door opened behind her as she passed. She didn't see the hand that reached in front of her until it was too late.

Chapter Sixteen

The rough skin of Clayton's palm scraped against Lindsey's mouth as he yanked her from the hall. She knew it was him before she heard his voice.

"Don't make a sound," his sick, raspy voice threatened.

Though the light was off, the unmistakable smells of bleach and urine revealed they were in a bathroom. He tightened his hold, pulling the back of her body against his. She stiffened and fought to keep from passing out, though it was hard to breathe with his hand covering her nose and mouth. *God, please don't let him hurt Samantha.*

The door eased shut on its vacuum hinge. "Today was a warning. I can make a stink. I can get custody of those girls." With the hand that held her, he trailed his fingers up her arm leaving an icy shiver. When she tried to squirm away they became hard as steel, bruising her skin. "Your sister told me how much you hated her addiction. The same thing will happen to her brats if you don't start filling that can."

Lindsey's heart pounded against her chest. Why was he doing this? He'd never been this persistent when Mike was alive. He thrust her to the side.

Lindsey's ankle buckled from the force. Her arms flailed through the air at nothing. With a crack, her head hit the tiled floor. Bright lights flashed through the darkness as if someone was flipping the light switch off and on. A cold sensation crawled from her shoulders to her head, pulling her into a lightless abyss.

Lindsey stirred and moaned. Her head felt like she'd met a train head-on. She curled into a ball. She was so cold. Her bed felt as hard as . . . the floor.

She blinked. An image of Clayton filled her mind. "Samantha!" Lindsey jumped to her feet in one quick motion. Her legs swayed and her head began to spin. She reached into the darkness and fumbled for something to hold on to. Her hand made contact with the curve of a sink. Lindsey grabbed its edge as her knees buckled beneath her. Kneeling, she rested her forehead against the cool porcelain and took a deep breath.

She forced her shaky legs to support her weight and felt along the wall. The darkness spun around her. Twice she had to pause and lean against the wall, willing the momentum of the room to stop. The desire to throw up made her gag. She couldn't get sick. There wasn't a second to spare!

The feel of wall paper changed to a smooth cool texture. The door. With a shove, she stumbled forward. The light of the hall temporally blinded her causing her to lose her balance. Someone steadied her by the arm.

"Are you okay, Miss?"

Lindsey pressed a hand against the pounding in her skull. "No, I have to check on my niece. Call the police. He was here."

The attendant looked confused and glanced down both ends of the hallway. "Ma'am, are you a patient here?"

Lindsey's voice rose. "Please get me to room 207. We have to hurry, my niece is in danger." Her words began to slur, the lights flickered off and on again. Then all went black.

She moaned and fluttered her eyelids until she could keep them open. A latex gloved hand moved over her face. A masked man shined a light in her eyes. Was this a nightmare?

"Lindsey. Lindsey, can you hear me?"

A frown furrowed her brow over her eyes but she managed to nod. She didn't understand why she was here.

"Other than an egg-size lump on her head, she'll be fine. She must have passed out in the lavatory."

Lavatory. Suddenly it all came back to her. "No." Her voice sounded weak. "I was pushed. My niece, Samantha . . ."

"Your niece is in her bed. We checked on her."

"You don't understand. I need the police. I need to see Samantha."

The doctor shook his head and looked toward a nurse. "She's not making sense. I'll sedate her so she can sleep—"

"No!" Lindsey found enough strength to push herself up and swung her legs off the table. "The man who drugged her was here. He threw me to the floor."

***

Samantha lay curled on her side. It had taken an exhausting twenty minutes to quiet her niece to sleep after the nurses had awakened her to check for injuries. Thankfully, it appeared Clayton had only wanted to threaten Lindsey. Samantha hadn't been touched. The poor child. She didn't understand what was happening or why she couldn't go home. Her screams still resounded in Lindsey's ears. She feared their lives would never again be normal. Even now, an armed policeman stood guard outside their door.

With gentle ease, so as not to wake the small girl, Lindsey slid to the side of Samantha's bed and stepped to the floor. The only way she'd calmed Samantha down was to curl up next to her. She didn't mind, but she couldn't stay there. Exhausted or not, Samantha tossed her limbs like a batter in a batting cage.

She reached for a tissue and paused. It wouldn't do any good. She couldn't get the smell of the hospital out of her sinuses until she went home. The sterile scent made her sick to her stomach. Images of Mike in his hospital bed assaulted her mind. She looked back at her niece. Healthy limbs reminded her of the difference of their injuries.

Lauren had once been in the same situation as her daughter, lying so quietly in a hospital bed. Lindsey and her sister had both been drilled by social workers, but neither of them would say anything against their parents. With stony-eyed silence, Lindsey had stared at the wall while the questions continued to hit close to home. She couldn't tell on her parents. They'd told her what would happen. That she and Lauren would be separated in different foster homes and never see each other again.

A clammy sensation tingled on Lindsey's hands and crept up her arms. Her light-headedness was back. Reaching her bed, she rolled onto the mattress and wished the merry-go-room would stop.

How long she'd slept, she didn't know. Lindsey turned over and stared at the phone. She longed to hear Keaton's voice tell her it would be okay, to feel the security of his strong arms. But the other children needed security, too, and to call him away would only upset them.

The dampness on her pillow revealed she'd been crying. It was a lonely life when you only had one person to depend on. She had Mike to thank for that. No doubt he had acted from the example set by his father, but how did someone justify such behavior? What was the harm in friendship?

Keaton encouraged her to have friends. He even brought over his sister with that intent.

Did Lucy know what had happened? She hoped to see her soon and explain she'd chased all doubts of marrying Keaton away.

Hours later, Lindsey stirred awake in response to voices outside her room. Keaton and the guard were arguing over why Samantha couldn't have visitors.

"Don't be crazy, Al, you know me."

"I'm sorry Keaton, but I have my orders."

Lindsey rushed to the door and through it open. Her quick movements still made her dizzy. She grabbed the frame of the door for support. Keaton pushed past Al and pulled her to him.

"I'm so glad you're here." She melted against him as his arms tightened around her, securing her heart to his.

"I missed you," he whispered in her hair. "How's our girl?"

Our girl. Like a flower opening in spring, warmth bloomed in Lindsey's heart. She smiled and stepped back, pulling him into the room despite the warning look on the guard's face. "Come and see."

Samantha had turned over in the night and now lay with her arms thrown over her head. Keaton stepped closer to her bed. "Will she be all right?" His question was whispered, as if he were afraid of what the answer might be.

"Yes. They said she could go home today." She stalled and pulled at her lip while still using him as support. "Something else happened last night, though. Clayton was here."

Keaton's eyes narrowed and moved from the window to the door. "That explains Al. What happened?"

Lindsey found herself back in Keaton's embrace before she finished the telling of the previous night. In such a short amount of time, he'd become her safe-haven. Never had someone shown so much concern for her or her children's lives.

***

Keaton carried Samantha through the front door and settled her on the couch. The children crowded around her like a new hen in a hen house.

Lindsey had worried her lip all the way home and was already searching for things to keep her busy. Keaton answered the children's questions while watching her gather laundry, open and close cupboards and sweep the floor. Finally, he could take no more.

"Lindsey." He wrapped his hand around her arm and pulled her to a kitchen chair "You're making me nervous. Calm down—we're home, I'm here with you." The phone rang and tore apart the false veil of security. The children stopped playing and looked toward Keaton. Lindsey's wide-eyed stare met his from across the table.

"I'll answer it." Keaton reached for the phone nearest him. "Hello?"

"This is Cooper down at the station. Is this you, Keaton?"

They knew one another from the sale barn. As was common in the area, most farmers held an extra job. "Yeah, it's me."

"Good. Stay on, but have Lindsey listen, too."

Keaton motioned for Lindsey to pick up the phone in the living room.

"I'm here." Her rattled nerves exposed themselves in the tremor of her voice.

"Just keeping you updated. We couldn't find any fingerprints on the package of candy from your house, so we don't have Clayton there. But if we can get lil' Sam to—"

"Samantha." An awkward silence followed. "She doesn't like to be called Sam. It makes her think people are calling her a boy."

Cooper cleared his throat. "Sorry 'bout that. But if Samantha will cooperate, we hope her description of who gave her the candy will match Clay's."

Lindsey sagged against the cushions of the couch and swiped at tears that slipped from her eyes. "So without that, we won't have any proof."

The officer sighed through the phone, "I'm sorry, but those are the facts."

Keaton thanked his friend and hung up the phone. He walked over to Lindsey and removed the phone from her hand and returned it to its cradle. "He can't be too smart. He'll make a slip-up soon enough."

Lindsey pulled Samantha next to her. "We have to know something, sweetie." Samantha nodded, her eyes fixed in a serious stare. "Who gave you the candy? Can you tell us what the person looked like?"

The child's eyes filled with tears. "Nobody. Me just found it."

Lindsey's brow furrowed. "What do you mean?'"

Samantha buried her head in Lindsey's chest. "I won't do it again." Her shoulders shook as she sobbed. "I find it on the shelf."

Keaton sighed and ran a hand through his hair. Without an I.D., Clayton couldn't be charged with the crime against Samantha. Nor could they charge him on breaking and entering.

He glanced at Lindsey and her niece. They were both exhausted. "Come on you two, you're going to bed." He slid his arms under Lindsey and cradled them both to his chest. Samantha stopped crying enough to reward him with a small giggle.

Lindsey tipped her head up. "Keaton, what are you doing?"

"Taking care of you. Hope you don't mind." Though it wasn't a full smile, the effort behind the tilt of her mouth struck a chord deep inside. He laid them on his bed and pulled the curtains. "Can I get anything for your headache?"

"No, I took something at the hospital. How'd you know I have a headache?"

He leaned over and kissed their foreheads and withheld his answer. She wouldn't like knowing the dark circles under her eyes had been the give-away. She was nearly asleep when her head hit his pillow.

"Before you're totally asleep, I want you to know Clara called for you as we were leaving last night. She said, *Mama*, and pointed at the hospital." He smiled at the angelic look in her eyes and slipped from the room.

Keaton poured himself a cup of coffee and shuffled through the mail and other various forms of paperwork that always littered his table. A sermon note-sheet slid from the pile. He recognized the name of the church as the one his sister attended. Skimming through the front page, the focus of the sermon had been on fasting.

The subject wasn't something often taught on. Lucy had added to the prepared notes to look up Matthew 17:21. Keaton's Bible sat on the nightstand in his bedroom. He didn't want to wake the girls. Instead he searched through the bookshelf in the front room. The book he pulled out wasn't the King James Version he was used to, but it would do.

Flipping through to Matthew, he trailed his finger along the verses. Verse 21 was missing. Keaton scrunched his brow and looked again. The chapter went from twenty to twenty two. Now his curiosity was peaked. He'd have to sneak into his bedroom for his Bible after-all.

He checked on the children playing upstairs then came back down and pushed his door open. Like a painted canvas, Lindsey and Samantha lay snuggled together as if sharing peaceful dreams. They looked so right nestled in his bed. Samantha's light brown hair blended with

Lindsey's darker tresses in a wave of softness. Soon they'd be his to snuggle with as well. He didn't know how long he stood staring, but when the thundering of footsteps sounded on the stairs, he knew he needed to retrieve what he came in for and close the door.

Once again settled at the kitchen table, Keaton flipped open his Bible. There it was, verse twenty one, *"Howbeit this kind goeth not out but by prayer and fasting."* In this particular passage, the disciples were having trouble casting out a devil from a man's son. Verse twenty-one was Jesus' answer as to them. He couldn't understand why it wasn't in the other version.

Keaton ran a hand over the back of his neck. If he were to think like his adversary, the devil, it made perfect sense. If fasting weakened the devil's powers, he'd find a way to hide the fact from God's people.

The pages flipped by in a blur as Keaton searched other areas for fasting. The Bible supported numerous accounts. Reasons varied from casting out devils to praying for guidance.

"Daddy!" Samantha ran toward him with open arms. The name from her lips resounded in his heart.

He swung her onto the table in front of him, scooting the books and paperwork aside. "Did you have a good nap with Mama?"

Her nod was quickly replaced by her tummy. At the sound of its growl she announced, "An' I'm hungry."

Lindsey walked up behind them and laughed. "Always."

Keaton followed her movements through the kitchen. Her skin had regained its healthy color. For that he was glad, but the single thought of her in the hands of Clayton turned his insides into a solid weight. The drug addict's actions were those of a coward— certainly no man of ethics would ever harm a woman or child.

The phone rang. Keaton lifted Samantha from the table to the chair and grabbed the receiver. "Hello."

"Mr. Durham, this is Ms. Roberts from DFS."

Chapter Seventeen

Keaton hung up the phone and met Lindsey's discouraged gaze. "Ms. Roberts will be here tomorrow evening." He couldn't stand the stress that weighed on Lindsey's shoulders. "I'll make sure I leave work on time. You won't have to deal with her on your own."

She crossed her arms and shrugged. "She's not so bad."

"Lindsey," Keaton didn't want to, but he had to prepare her, "without fingerprints, all we have to go on is the recording from his phone call. That may not be enough to convince her . . ."

Her shoulders began to shake. She dropped her head to her chin to hide the tears that tumbled down her cheeks. Keaton's heart broke. In two long strides he was by her side. He wrapped her in his embrace. Stroking her back, he prayed out loud. "Lord, comfort us all through this trial. Please open Ms. Roberts' eyes to the truth and keep our—*this* family together."

Lindsey wasn't yet his. He didn't want to scare her away by assuming too much. She pulled back and wiped her eyes. "Thank you, Keaton." She turned toward the stove. "I'd better start dinner."

He wanted to tell her he'd cook, that she should rest, but he understood her need for something to do. He felt it too. "I'll mow the yard."

Keaton told the kids to stay in the front yard while he mowed in back. They all consented but Jack. He followed him around like a shadow. "Is something on your mind?"

"Mom's scared, isn't she?"

"Yeah."

"You won't let that woman take us away, will you?"

The worry in Jack's eyes formed a lump in Keaton's throat. He knelt to eye level and put a hand on Jack's shoulder. "I've got a direct line to God. With His help, we're all going to stay together."

Jack wrapped his arms around Keaton's neck and squeezed. "I love you. I'm glad you're my dad."

"Me, too, Bud." Keaton returned the hug and blinked furiously to keep tears from giving away his soft heart. "Now, why don't you help me out by getting that gas can and we'll fill the mower?"

An hour later, hands had been washed and everyone was seated around the table. The meal Lindsey had prepared in such a short time would impress a five-star chef. Chicken baked with onion, garlic, apples and potatoes created a stir with almost everyone, especially Keaton's stomach. As soon as he stepped into the kitchen the smell made his stomach growl loud enough to make the children laugh.

Samantha scrunched up her nose. "Bummer. Me wanted hammenburgs!"

186

Lindsey smiled and shook her head. "Then you should have told me, because I would've fixed them."

"Fixed *what?*" Keaton slanted his head toward Samantha hoping to better hear if she repeated the foreign word.

"That's Samantha's way of saying hamburgers."

He glanced at the healthy bundle of energy, thankful for her presence at the table.

***

Lindsey washed down the chairs and table while Keaton kept the children busy outside with a game of freeze-tag. She brushed away a tear that slipped from the corner of her eye. No matter what she did her mind continued to replay yesterday's events.

In the store, she had counted the children and one was missing. If she'd kept a closer eye on them, she could've saved her niece from putting the candy in her mouth. She should have at least noticed Samantha was sucking on something when she buckled her in the booster-seat. Arguable facts swam through her mind but she refused to rationalize them. It didn't matter that she had six children to keep up or that Bradley had needed a restroom or that Clara constantly clung to her.

Lindsey needed to feel responsible. Guilt gave her a form of control. It meant that Clayton didn't hold all the cards. That next time, she would do better. Next time, she would pay more attention.

Tears closed off her throat. Pressure built behind her eyes until her head throbbed. A hiccup was all it took. She broke down and sobbed. Leaning on the table for support, she allowed her heart to release a portion of its pain.

Guilt also meant she had failed.

Her shoulders shook with more emotion. Social services might think she'd failed, too. Surveillance she could deal with, but if they tried to take her children . . . they might put them in temporary foster care. That would set Clara back more than before. She may never learn to talk.

A fork fell to the floor. She bent to retrieve it. Her throat constricted. She gagged and rushed to the trash can. Like a noose, fear tightened around her neck, squeezing the life from her. She had to get control before her stress caused real sickness.

Keaton knew. She could see it in his eyes. He was worried for her. But he struggled with the same battle. He loved her children. After the call from D.F.S., she watched him debate what to do. She'd been afraid he was going to insist on cooking. Relief had eased the tension in her shoulders when he settled for mowing. He needed an outlet, too. It was amazing how similar they were.

The rest of the evening passed quickly leaving them upstairs to tuck the children into their sleeping bags. After they said good night, Lindsey paused outside their door. "I'm so scared I'll lose them."

Keaton drew her to him. "Shh, you won't lose them. Don't talk like that."

She drew in a deep breath but hiccuped again. Tears formed as big wet balls, hovering on the edge of her eyes. One blink sent them tumbling over each other, wetting through Keaton's cotton shirt.

He moved his arm from around her and slipped it under her knees, lifting her off the floor. At the bottom of the steps, he sat down and cradled her in his arms. She looked up. His eyes were closed and his mouth moved in silent words.

"What are you doing?"

He opened his eyes. Moisture glistened on top of shimmering depths of blue. "Praying for you."

Again, his thoughtfulness struck a chord deep inside. Had Mike ever prayed for her? Only in mockery. She wiped her eyes and leaned her head against his shoulder. She prayed a silent prayer of her own.

***

The morning passed with the speed of a turtle. A box-turtle to be exact. Squatted in the grass next to Josh and Bradley, with Clara on her hip, Lindsey watched two turtles race one another to a strawberry. From the length of her shortening shadow, it seemed that neither reptile had been informed they were in a race.

She finally stood and switched Clara to her other hip. "Okay boys, it's about lunch time. I'm going to have to give my stadium seats to someone else."

Elizabeth and Samantha shook their heads as they walked past. "Not us," Elizabeth said, "we think their pets are boring."

Samantha spun around in circles. "I'm hungry. What me going to eat?"

"How about a picnic at the creek?" Ann's voice came from behind. Lindsey turned around to see her carrying a basket so full its lid wouldn't clasp.

The children cheered with the idea while Clara clapped bringing a smile to Lindsey's face. She'd missed her quiet sidekick while at the hospital. "That sounds great. I'll get the drinks."

Lindsey walked beside Ann, listening as she involved the children in conversation. Encouraging their questions and asking many of her own. If Donna had ever interacted with them, they might ask about her and Mike. But it seemed they were never missed. None of her children had mentioned their grandparents since their return overseas.

At the creek, she helped Ann unpack the basket while the children splashed in the water. Disturbed by their presence, a blue jay squawked overhead while two robins flitted from tree to tree, indifferent to the new company.

Lindsey sighed with contentment. It appeared they'd stepped off the canvas of a Norman Rockwell painting and sprang to life. She hummed the tune that Sleeping Beauty sang while in the woods and imagined dancing between the trees. If only she could live in this moment.

She saw Ann glance her direction and smile. What wonderful parents Keaton had. And what wonderful in-laws they would be. Butterflies fluttered in her abdomen. Despite all that had taken place, her mind often dwelled on the thought of becoming Keaton's bride.

The image of him running back to the house in the rain teased her senses. She slowed the snapshots of her memories as she pictured him pulling his wet shirt over his head. One of her favorite memories. Clara's laugh drew her back to the present.

Clara wiggled her toes out of the pile of sand where Bradley had them buried. She laughed again and hugged her shoulder to her cheek. The sight of her happiness squeezed Lindsey's heart, and evidently Ann's. Ann stepped closer to Lindsey and spoke softly, "I think that girl is going to change one day very soon. You'll put her to bed in her silent little way and in the morning she'll be talking about everything."

Lindsey pulled at her lip. "I hope you're right." Thoughts of Division of Family Services worried her mind.

"Come on, kids, let's pray." Ann reached for Lindsey's hand. Her eyes bore through her. "Don't worry. We're in God's hands."

Ann had outdone herself in the eyes of the children. Sandwiches of peanut butter and strawberry, freezer jam couldn't be beat. Brownies and cookies followed, all homemade. Lindsey reached for another cookie even though she was ready to pop. "These are so good. You'll have to share your recipe."

"I already planned to. Actually, I'll let you in on your surprise."

Lindsey scrunched her brows. "*My* surprise?"

"A wedding present from me to you." She held up a hand to stop Lindsey's protest. "I'm making a recipe scrapbook of all Keaton's favorite dishes. I was always told the way to a man's heart was through his stomach." She tapped a finger to her chin. "But I think Keaton proved differently."

"What do you mean?"

"As his mama, I've waited a long time to see my son fall in love. There are those that tried to snag him with their cooking at church socials. Some that tried to share his interests. And some that I tried to match him with myself. Never a good idea, by the way." She rolled her eyes and sighed, seemingly at disastrous memories.

Then she laughed and shook her head. "All those wasted efforts when it was really quite simple. All it took," Ann ran a hand over Lindsey's hair in a motherly fashion, "was you."

A sheen of moisture glistened in Ann's eyes. Lindsey leaned into her as she drew her in a sideways hug. "Jacob and I thank God every day for you and your kids. We're so happy to soon be grandparents to them."

Lindsey straightened and fiddled with the hem of her shirt. "Why are you so confident we'll get married? I haven't . . ."

"You will." Ann stood and cleaned up their leftover meal. "You both walk around with stars in your eyes, whether you're together or merely thinking of the other." She winked and took Clara's hand to join the others in the creek.

Lindsey stood to follow but tripped over her own feet. She caught a branch to keep from falling. Was it that obvious? A smile stretched across her face as tingles tickled her shoulders and head.

Love. The beginning of fairy-tales.

"Mama, look at that fish. He's not swimming no-where." Samantha pulled on Lindsey's cut-offs and pointed a few feet away.

"That's weird." Lindsey stepped into the creek and watched the minnow flap on its side. It didn't move with the current. She stepped closer. The water rippled. "Snake!"

She splashed over rocks as she grabbed her niece and motioned with her hand. "Get out, get out of the water!"

"No, stay where you are." Ann's quiet control caused Lindsey to pause.

"You don't understand—"

Ann laughed good-heartedly. "Look again at your snake."

She turned and peered closer. Where had it gone? Closer to the bank, its head broke the surface again. The soft shelled turtle lumbered out of the water onto a log and gulped down the fish. The children laughed and chanted, "Mom's afraid of a turtle!"

Lindsey released her breath and laughed in return. "Yeah, yeah, so I over-reacted."

Ann patted her arm. "Good call though if it had been a snake. I always did the same thing when my kids were young. Never have gotten used to things that slither. Though I did have a code word I used. Do you have one?"

"A code word?"

Ann nodded. "To signal for danger. Ours was tomcat. If I hollered, they knew to get to safety."

Lindsey couldn't hide her smile. She tried to picture Ann yelling tomcat and the children taking her seriously.

Ann laughed at herself. "Well, you wouldn't have to use my word. You could choose your own. But it's something to consider."

"Let's do it, Mom!" Jack corralled the others to agree.

"Okay then. What do you think would make a good word?"

"Speed Racer."

"Yeah, that's a good one."

The boys had agreed but the girls seemed less than enthused. But for whatever reason, it stuck. "Speed Racer it is."

***

Keaton's stomach rumbled and reminded him to pray. He'd avoided food all day in an effort to fast. "God," he spoke softly in prayer as he walked to his vehicle, "please take away Lindsey's fears. Give her hope and reassure her that You're in control. Keep her children with her and . . ." He paused as he had all day when it came to the next part of his prayer. But as Jesus instructed, he asked, "Please show Clayton his need for repentance."

Praying for one's enemies wasn't something that came easy in this instance. He continued to list other needs until someone hollered at him from somewhere in the parking lot. Keaton turned to see Denton running toward him.

"Hey, I just wanted to tell you I enjoyed working with you these past months. I thought for sure you'd be the man they wanted though."

Denton had received the promotion of manager today and was on cloud nine. "You're a good man to work with, Denton. You'll make us a fine manager. Congratulations."

"Thanks, Keaton. Now I can afford my kid's braces." He waved good-bye as he turned back to the building. "Gotta get back and fix a machine."

Keaton watched him go, glad it wasn't him.

Half an hour later, he saw Ms. Roberts to the table as Lindsey poured them all a cup of coffee. The children had said their hellos and withstood the standard prodding for information as though their visitor was innocently curious. They now lingered just outside the kitchen, their nosy personalities keeping them from play.

The social worker sighed heavily then focused her attention. "Lindsey, I know you've been through a lot, and I hate to be the bearer of bad news, but since there weren't any prints found on the candy or any way to prove your statement, you're going to be seeing a lot more of me."

Chapter Eighteen

Lindsey sat quietly with her hands wrapped around her cup, staring at the swirl of dark brew. Ms. Roberts continued, "I have a note here about the children's attire at the hospital. They hadn't appeared bathed. Can you tell me about that?"

Keaton ground his teeth and ran a hand through his hair. Had the woman married and had children, perhaps she'd understand every day didn't fall into a set standard. Some went like clockwork while most didn't. And others left you wanting to hammer something. He'd only been around the family less than two months and had learned that.

Lindsey spoke up and drew his attention. "The children had been playing outside and friends from church stopped by and offered the use of their van. The kids were so excited to go to town I figured baths could wait until later. It's not my norm, but that's what we did. I can't control how you interpret it."

Ms. Roberts slanted her head and looked puzzled. "Lindsey, I'm not accusing you. This is standard questioning. The call that was originally made suggested there was abuse in the household and possible drug usage. I've found nothing, thus far, to substantiate it, but I still have a job to do."

Keaton reached for Lindsey's hand. He wanted to convey he was on her side and he knew she could never be like her parents. Lindsey drew in a deep breath. "Have you spoken with the police?"

"About what?"

Keaton could tell the social worker hadn't heard about Lindsey's attack at the hospital. He glanced to his side. Lindsey paled, her hand trembled beneath his.

"I'll explain." Keaton gave a short description based on what Lindsey had shared with him. Ms. Roberts scribbled in her note sheet to keep up.

As expected, she questioned them further for another twenty minutes. Keaton saw her glance at her empty coffee cup a couple of times but didn't offer to fill it. If she were thirsty, let her take the hint and go home. She'd put Lindsey through enough.

Ms. Roberts snapped the cap back on her pen and returned it to her bag. "One more question to bring this evening to an end. What exactly is the relationship between you two?"

Keaton again found himself wanting to show the woman out the door. She had a way of irritating him to the extreme. What business was it of hers?

Lindsey explained their situation with simple tact. "Keaton was my late husband's friend. He stays at his parents' house across the road at night and, until we feel safe enough to go home, he lets us stay here."

As though not convinced it was all so pure, Ms. Roberts gave a mocking glance between them. "And there's no romantic entanglement here?"

"Sure there is." It was Keaton's turn. And he intended to end it. "I've fallen in love with Lindsey and her kids. And I hope to convince her to marry me." He watched the woman's face change expressions as quick as the tide. "Satisfied?"

"Very. As I told you earlier, I'm not here to accuse either of you. I happen to believe everything you've told me is the truth." She looked at Keaton, "I'm also glad you've recognized what I saw in our first visit." Turning to Lindsey, she added, "And I hope you recognize it, too."

Ms. Roberts gathered her file of paperwork and headed for the door. Keaton and Lindsey followed with the children circled around them, like any regular family. They stopped at the door and Samantha stepped closer to Ms. Roberts and tugged on her hand. She squatted to eye level. "Yes, sweetie?"

Samantha's voice came out whispered. "He used to make my first mommy cry."

Ms. Roberts glanced at Keaton and back to her. "Who did, honey?"

"The scary man. He came to my room when Mama wasn't there."

Keaton's blood turned cold.

A moan sounded from Lindsey then she fainted against him.

***

Lindsey stirred on the couch and felt someone's warmth next to her. She blinked and opened her eyes, it was Keaton. He removed a wet cloth from her forehead. His eyes shone with concern.

"What happened?"

"You passed out, dear." Ms. Roberts squatted beside her. The children sat in various places in the room, all eyes on her.

Then it came back. Samantha. Clayton had been to her room. Panic rose in her chest. How could she keep her safe?

"Easy there, Lindsey. Take slow, deep breaths." Keaton's soothing voice had a calming effect on her soul.

Samantha crowded to Ms. Roberts' side. The woman smiled at her and gave a light hug. "Your mama is going to be fine."

"He said me going to live with him." Tears filled her eyes. "Me want to stay here."

Pain sliced through Lindsey's heart as her niece's lips began to quiver. She held out her arms. "Come here, sweetie." She cradled her close. "I'll never let you go. You're mine and always will be."

Samantha cuddled closer and reached a hand out to touch Keaton's arm. "And me yours, too."

He leaned over to kiss her head. "That's right."

Nobody pressed her further. Ms. Roberts gave the signal not to. If anything else needed to be told, Samantha would do it on her own time. For now she needed security.

They directed the children to brush their teeth and spoke with the social worker by the door. Lindsey asked the question that had been haunting her. "Is it possible for Clayton to get custody of the girls?"

"If he wants to pursue his rights, you'll have a tough battle to win. All you have on him is a taped phone call which may not be allowed in court. It would be difficult, if not next to impossible, to prove he said anything."

Lindsey held a trembling hand over her mouth. She wanted to scream at the injustice.

"Honey, all I'm saying is if he is in fact the children's father, he has parental rights. Now if he isn't, or if it's never been stated legally that he's their father, then a DNA test would have to be administered."

Keaton pulled her close. "And the good thing about that is he'd never want to have it done. His blood would show he wasn't clean."

Ms. Roberts smiled and nodded her head. "Most likely." She patted Lindsey's arm. "I wouldn't be too concerned at this point. From all I've heard, I doubt he's serious."

She may have said the words, but the woman couldn't hide the concern from her eyes. Did she share Lindsey's fears that Clayton might try to steal Samantha? She sighed heavily and leaned into Keaton's strong support.

After Ms. Roberts left, she and Keaton said good-night prayers with the children then it was time for Keaton to say good-night as well. Lindsey loved his shy-boy look. Standing in the doorway with his brows drawn up in the form of a roof-top, he looked so charming. But as she'd always known, Keaton possessed something more than charm. Truth and honesty. And from the way his eyes darkened, a deep attraction to her.

Lindsey easily succumbed to his open arms.

"I love you, Lindsey." His whispered testament sent shivers all the way to her toes. She turned her head to meet his lips. Their warmth seared a path straight to her heart.

She couldn't wait until they were married.

A fire started in the pit of her stomach. Keaton deepened their kiss. Fragments of emotions left from the evening added to the intensity, building their passion. She pulled closer, wanting his security, his protection, his love to swallow her whole. He released her lips, but her fingers found their way through his tousled hair capturing him to her again. It had been so long since she desired any form of intimacy.

But it had to stop. They weren't married.

She pulled back and instantly felt the loss of Keaton's warmth. His mouth pulled at the side. Flames danced in his eyes as they trailed from her face to her hair but careful to stop before devouring too much.

He stepped through the door. "I'll be out here if you need me."

Lindsey leaned through the doorway and watched as he crowded his legs on the swing and stretched his arms over his head. She loved loving him.

Tiny footsteps sounded behind her. Lindsey turned to find Samantha had climbed out of bed and came downstairs. "What's wrong, sweetie?"

"Where's Daddy?"

"Right outside. Do you need to see?"

Samantha nodded her head and followed through the door Lindsey held open. "Stay with us, pleassseee." Samantha tugged on Keaton's arm. He reached down and picked her up. As he hugged her close, his eyes stayed on Lindsey. "I'll be right outside in this swing."

Samantha pulled back. "But why can't you sleep with Mommy?"

Lindsey felt heat rise to her face. Keaton's eyes seemed to darken before he pulled them from her and concentrated on the girl in his arms. "Because if I sleep outside, Samson can tell me if anyone comes to visit."

Solemn eyes nodded in understanding. Such youth should never have to know—

Lindsey frowned. The swing was too narrow for Keaton. He didn't look at all comfortable. "Please come inside." Knowing he would never take his bedroom from her, she added, "You can sleep on the couch."

His mouth spread in a slow smile as he took in her full appearance. "I'd be too tempted not to stay put."

Her jaw dropped open. Then a smile, she couldn't hide, claimed her mouth. "Come on, Samantha. Let's all go to bed. Daddy will keep us safe."

Daddy. The word melted like sugar on her tongue.

***

Lindsey kept pace beside Lucy as they walked down the gravel road. Ann had insisted on watching the children, giving the girls time to talk. She squirmed under Lucy's intense gaze.

"Tell me something. Why did you marry Mike?"

"He told me he'd accepted a job in Missouri. Two days later he took me to the courthouse where I became his wife."

Lucy slowly shook her head. "Didn't you want a real wedding?"

"You have to understand I needed to get away. My family was heavy into drugs. By that, I mean they were always under the influence and more than once offered it to me and my sister." Lindsey stared across the field. Though cattle grazed in a dot to dot pattern, she only saw memories she never liked to visit. "Mike never asked me to marry him. He just told me that's what we were doing."

Lucy seemed to understand her hesitation about the past. She grasped her hand and swung it with hers. "So, when are you and Keaton getting married?"

Lindsey laughed then grew serious. "He hasn't asked recently."

"You mean he hasn't asked again since you decided to say yes?"

Lindsey shrugged. "Well, yes."

"He'll ask."

She worried her lip. "Tomorrow's already September. I only have two weekends left."

Lucy smiled and turned her head away. Did she know something Lindsey didn't?

From their short time as friends, Lindsey had already learned Lucy could be more than stubborn. If she did know something, it wouldn't do any good trying to pry it from her. Lindsey turned the conversation to something else.

"The kids are missing their toys. I'm going to have to go back to the house soon."

"You don't mean go back as in, move back in, do you?"

She shrugged. "That depends on your brother." A satisfied grin claimed Lucy's mouth before Lindsey continued. "Regardless, the children do need some things, school books for one. We've enjoyed our vacation but it's time to get back to business."

"Did you know Mom home-schooled us?"

"No. I guess Keaton and I never got around to discussing it." A worry she hadn't been aware of loosened its hold on her heart. "So Ann wouldn't object to me schooling the kids?"

"Why would she? They're your kids."

"Mike's parents hate the idea. They even want me to get rid of Samantha and Clara."

Lucy stopped so fast her heels skidded in the gravel. "What?"

"Don't worry, Lucy. I would never, ev-er, give up any of my children. And my nieces are just as much mine as the four I gave birth to."

"I don't know your in-laws, but I already don't like them."

"Then pray for them with me."

Lucy shook her head. "You've got a stronger faith than me, girl. How do you do it? I mean, with your husband's illness and death, your in-laws' lack of support, Clayton looming over you. How can you still talk about prayer and keep your faith intact?"

"By digging deep into God's word. I'll admit I don't have a lot of time. But what I can find, I try to make it stick. Like yesterday morning at the hospital. Someone brought me a Bible to read from the chapel and I've already memorized some verses that stuck out.

"Rejoice in the Lord always; and again I say, Rejoice. Let your moderation be known unto all men. The Lord is at hand. Be careful for nothing, but in everything by prayer and supplication with thanksgiving let your requests be made known unto God." Lindsey's heart warmed toward the last verse. "And the peace of God, which passeth all understanding, shall keep your hearts and minds through Christ Jesus."

"Wow for two reasons. One, that you memorized all of that. And two, those are powerful verses."

Lindsey watched Lucy from the corner of her eye as they walked back to the cabin. What was going through her mind and what was keeping her from having the same kind of faith?

They reached Keaton's house where Ann had the children lined up playing ball. She excused herself and stepped toward them. "Lindsey, you got a call from somebody named, Donna."

Chapter Nineteen

Lindsey had no idea how Donna had gotten Keaton's number, unless she'd remembered his name and called information. Still, why had she called? Guilt formed as a headache above her eye. Had something happened to her younger son, Bryan? She hoped not. To lose both sons would be too much to ask anyone to bear.

The world weighed on her mind. She didn't have their number with her, it was at home. She pulled out a piece of paper and wrote down all the items needed from her house. Whether it was safe or not, a trip had to be made.

"Lindsey?" Ann walked into the kitchen. "There you are. Are you all right?" She peered over her shoulder. "Oh no. You're not thinking of going there by yourself, are you?"

Heat rose to her cheeks, thankfully she didn't color easily. "Uh, no. I'm only making a list for when I do go back I won't forget anything." It wasn't a lie. Of course she wanted to jump in the van and get the things that would make them more comfortable. But her sensibilities would have stopped her long before she left the drive.

Ann placed a hand over hers. "Good. I wouldn't want to risk losing you." After an extra squeeze, she left the room, but not before Lindsey noticed the tears that had gathered in her eyes.

Her chest expanded with emotion. It must have been heavenly to grow up with the security of Ann and Jacob as parents. Ann showed her the compassionate concern of a mother while Jacob provided a father's protectiveness, even if it was in his own quiet way.

Keaton's voice sounded through the screen door. It was Friday. He was home for the weekend. A fountain of excitement started in her toes and bubbled upward. His presence brought more happiness than she'd ever experienced from Mike. She hurried through the house only to slow as she neared the porch.

The front yard revealed happy children squealing in delight as Keaton and his dog chased them in circles. Another Rockwell moment. Lindsey sighed, "Let it last, Lord. Let it last."

She stepped through the door and stood with his mom and sister. Jacob drove up in his farm truck and the children left *Dad* for *Pa*. He leaned out the window where the children already clamored for attention. "I'm looking for some orphans to help me check my cattle." Lindsey laughed with her kids and helped them climb into the truck. As she stepped back, she bumped into Keaton. Their eyes met and everything else seemed to fade.

She heard a deep chuckle come from Jacob before he backed up, leaving them alone. Lindsey looked around. "Where's Ann and Lucy."

Keaton pointed to the back of the truck as it drove through the field. She hadn't even realized the women had climbed in, too.

Keaton stepped closer, his lips only a whisper away. "What should we do with our free time?"

Her pulse accelerated. What did he have in mind? She knew him too well to think he would try anything dishonorable. A small amount of disappointment shamed her. But when would he ask for her hand again? They only had two weeks left.

"Let's have some fun. You want crawfish for dinner?"

Lindsey's mind struggled to change her train of thought. Weren't craw fish the same thing as crawdads–like the kind that pinched her son's finger?

Keaton led her to a different section of the creek than she'd been to before. "I haven't gathered any all summer, so we should find an easy mess of them here, especially with the water being low."

Lindsey worried her lip with her bottom teeth. "How will we catch them?"

Keaton opened the lid of the minnow bucket and withdrew a small net. "We lift rocks and net or grab them."

"I'll net. You grab."

An hour later, the whole family feasted together on their catch. Jack insisted on sitting beside Jacob. He took a growing interest in the scar on Jacob's temple and those that covered his arms. Lindsey knew what was coming, but her curiosity kept her from distracting him.

"Pa Pa, how'd you get those?" His long finger, so much like Mike's, pointed to Jacob's arms.

Jacob looked from Jack to Ann, as if to get the okay. "A long time ago, we had a problem with a big, wild cat."

Lindsey became so engrossed in Jacob's tale of fighting a mountain lion she didn't realize Keaton had stepped away from the table to answer the phone. He returned and stood by his chair, waiting for his dad to finish.

Jacob wrapped up his story quicker than Lindsey would've preferred. "What is it, Son?"

Keaton looked across the table and met Lindsey's gaze. "That was Officer Cooper. It seems Clayton was involved in a hit and run two days ago and they haven't been able to find him. He hasn't shown up at his latest place of employment or his house."

A smile lit his eyes. "He's left town rather than face charges."

Lindsey held her breath in hopes it meant what she thought it did. Keaton nodded. "He's no longer a threat, Lindsey."

***

Lindsey pulled into the driveway of her house. Two weeks had passed since they'd come home to the broken window. She'd begun to wonder if it would ever be safe to return. Cooper had continued to patrol the area in search of Clayton and was convinced they were out of the risk of danger.

Lucy opened the back door of the van to release the excited children. Samantha tumbled out. "I'm going to get my dolly!"

Josh slid out after her. "I'm getting my truck.'"

Lindsey met them at the door. The dead-bolt turned over with a resounding click. Satisfied, she pushed it open and entered first. The house smelled funny after being cooped up. Stale air, mixed with odors from the kitchen, made her rush to open a window. Everyone followed closely behind her as they went room to room assuring their safety before they relaxed. Although Officer Cooper had checked on the house, she didn't want to leave anything to chance.

"Okay kids, gather what you want to take and put it by the door. Then you can play while I clean up."

Although she'd mentioned moving back in, Keaton and his family had talked her out of it. Their advice had been sound. Clayton may be gone now, but if he knew she was alone, he might take advantage and come back to demand money.

"Okay, girl, where can I start?" Lucy had readily agreed to come along and help. Lindsey knew the real reason was to give everyone peace of mind that she wouldn't be alone. Since it was already Wednesday, Ann was helping at the food pantry otherwise she would have found an excuse to join them, too.

"I need to clean out the fridge. After two weeks of being gone, I'm not sure what's growing in there. How about you help the kids? I don't want them trying to take their whole toy box."

Lindsey moved to the hallway and paused. The sight of her dishwasher brought back fond memories. The bubble incident was the first time Clara had laughed and the first time she'd felt Keaton's touch. A contented sigh escaped her. She was glad he'd talked her out of staying here. After spending so much time with him on his farm, this house could never again feel like home.

Entering the kitchen, she took a breath and held it as she opened the refrigerator.

What little milk was left had soured and owned at least partial responsibility for the foul smell. Lindsey threw it in the trash can and realized it also was a contributor. "Ugh, I shouldn't have left like this."

After cleaning out old food containers and soaking them in the sink, she collected trash from the other rooms then returned to the kitchen where Elizabeth stood with Clara, looking in the fridge.

"Mama, can I have an apple?"

"Sure, they're still good. Let me cut them in slices for everyone."

Lucy had stepped in and curled her nose. "Why'd you leave the seeds in?"

"They're good for you. I read if you eat them with the fruit, they fight gum disease and cavities."

"Hmm, I have a good dentist. I'll take mine without, thank you."

Clara held out one of her slices toward Lucy. "Here go."

Lindsey gasped and threw a hand over her heart. "Baby, you spoke!" She grabbed her from the chair and swirled her in the air. Clara laughed and squealed. Finally, she was growing beyond her past. *Thank you, Jesus.*

The other children ran in to share the excitement. Their genuine enthusiasm showed such beautiful support. She glanced at Lucy to share the moment and saw a tear slip from her eye. Again, she found herself thanking Jesus. Where would she be without Him and the Durhams?

After the apples were eaten and the children's hunger satiated for a while longer, she and Lucy concentrated on gathering school supplies while the children played. Lucy packed a box full of books while Lindsey gathered pencils and colors.

Lucy paused and looked around. "Do you miss this house?"

She choked out a laugh. "Are you kidding? It's falling apart around me. You saw me working with the clogged sink. Those dishes may still be in the water next time I stop by." She kicked the peeling linoleum with her toe. "When Mike bought it I argued it wasn't fit for us to live in. He said. . . well, it doesn't matter."

"Sure it matters. What did he say?"

Lindsey shrugged. "He said he bought it to teach me humility. That I was too vain, and he knew I'd think I deserved better."

Lucy shook her head, obviously biting her tongue. "How did you manage to deal with it?"

"I'd just remind myself a house doesn't make a home, it's the people in it."

"Again, I marvel at your faith. I hope I'm never tested to that extreme."

"I thought your husband was like Mike."

"He was in a way . . . but different."

Lindsey wanted to pry for more information, but Lucy didn't appear to want to expand on her late husband. It always seemed that way.

"Mom, we're hungry." Jack entered with his siblings. She almost laughed at their contorted faces. Left for an hour without food and they always thought they were starving. They didn't know how good they had it.

"We're out of food. I'd offer you peanut butter sandwiches but the bread got moldy." They moaned. "If you can hang on for one more hour, we'll be done and ready to go home."

"But we don't want to go home, yet, we still want to play." The boys had just finished setting up Mike's old train set and wanted time to enjoy it.

Lucy held up a hand. "I have an idea. Why don't I run in for pizza? My treat. I'll bring it back and we can eat it here while we finish up."

"Can me go, too?" Samantha ran to the door.

Clara reached for Lucy and bobbed her head up and down. "Ride. Ride."

Lindsey certainly couldn't refuse now. Whatever made her little one want to talk, she wanted to give in. "Okay. We'll be here when you get back."

***

With phone in hand, Lindsey sat across from the children's train set and dialed overseas. The time difference always baffled her. She could never remember what Donna's time was compared to hers. Hopefully it wouldn't start their conversation off on a wrong note.

The phone was answered on the second ring. "Donna?" Lindsey prayed it wasn't Mike who'd picked up.

Her mother-in-law cleared her throat. "Lindsey? Just a minute, let me step in the other room."

"Sorry if I woke you."

"No, don't be. I've wanted to talk to you but it's better if Michael doesn't wake up."

"How's Bryan?"

"Fine, why do you ask?"

213

Lindsey sighed with relief. "When you called at Keaton's, I was afraid something had happened."

"Hmm." Donna grew quiet. "That was thoughtful." Again, she was quiet for a moment. "I haven't been able to reach you, so I called information."

Lindsey wasn't sure what to say. She stalled for time. "I'm glad Bryan is doing well."

"But are you?"

Donna's concern surprised her. Pushing aside the worry of doubt that it might not be genuine, Lindsey dove into telling her about Clayton and the incident with Samantha. She'd never know of the woman's intentions until she opened up.

"Honey," Donna's voice broke, "I'm so sorry." She softly cried before sniffing and regaining her voice. "I don't know what to say, other than I'm glad they still have you."

Lindsey's mouth dropped open. She pulled the receiver back from her ear. It seemed to be working okay. She replaced it as Donna began to say something else.

"I'm sure Michael will eventually come around. I've realized that you're not me. I should never have been so outspoken with you when we were there. I hope you understand the stress we were under."

It wasn't an apology, but it would probably be the closet to one she was going to get. "I realize that, Donna."

"Will you be okay? You don't think that man will bother you again, do you?"

"No. The police said he left town. And Keaton's family keeps a close eye on us."

Donna cleared her throat. "Well . . . I think in light of all that's going on, it would be in your best interest to go ahead with that marriage."

For some reason, her last comment didn't soothe as much as her earlier ones had. Lindsey rubbed her forehead. She wasn't marrying Keaton just to be protected. She was marrying him because she'd fallen in love. But she knew better to waste an explanation on Donna. It was best to leave things as they were.

She thanked her for her concern and promised to keep in touch. The children continued to play, undisturbed that she'd hung up with their grandmother and no one was given the chance to talk with her.

Fifteen minutes later, her children's voices floated through the window in the kitchen as she again tried her effort with the clogged sink. A crack in the aged plunger did little to assist her. She paused and watched the kids sword fight imaginary dragons. It seemed odd to only count four heads. Her nieces had nestled a place in her heart alongside her children and though they were with someone she fully trusted, she still would rather them all be together.

Her eyes drew to the Butterfly Milkweed Keaton had mowed around. True to his word, the plant had bloomed into beautiful orange blossoms and attracted a myriad of colorful butterflies. She could see them perfectly from her kitchen window.

"This is not working." Lindsey tossed the plunger into the trash can and bent to rummage under the sink for anything that might prove more useful.

"Hey, kids, is your pretty momma home?" The familiar, raspy voice filtered through the window screen.

A drain cleanser dropped from Lindsey's hands as she stood and stared across the yard. She hoped her eyes wouldn't confirm who her ears told her was   there.

Chapter Twenty

Clayton Turnbaugh stood in front of her fear-stricken children. His head turned. Narrow eyes bore her direction. With the determination of a hunting cat, he stalked toward her. The bright orange flower crumpled beneath his feet. Butterflies scattered to safety.

"Hey, Sis, we have something to discuss."

She swallowed the hysteria his presence brought and fought for a controlled voice. "Kids," she yelled through the screen, "Speed Racer."

She prayed they knew to run for help. They had a neighbor up the road who was usually home.

Jack stood tall and brave in front of his siblings. She could count on him to try to protect them. But would he also think he could protect her? She hoped not, he didn't stand a chance.

Clayton stepped with confident strides toward the back door, his steady, unnerving gaze never wavered from where she stood. A fearful dread shivered through her.

If she ran, he'd only grab a child and use him or her against her. Lindsey's blood chilled as she fought against growing tremors.

He opened the door with all the ease of one used to entering her house. She backed against the sink wishing instead she could hide in a closet like when she was a child. But she was now the adult, and she couldn't allow him to hurt her children. Her hands fumbled for something to use in defense. Where was the knife she'd used on the apples?

A mocking sneer added to his sinister stare. He stepped closer, until his pitted skin was all she could see. The heat of his breath fanned her face. "You think you're too good to help me out, don't you?"

His gaze drifted toward the window. "I didn't see my girls out there. You hidin' them in here?"

Dull eyes searched her face. "It don't matter. I'll find them," his hand curled around her throat, "and your money."

Icy tendrils of fear snaked their way down her spine invading the tiny invisible hairs of her skin. The offensive smell of his body began to fade as his hand tightened. This couldn't be the end. She had to break free. Lindsey gasped and kicked, but his body was pressed too close.

His grip on her throat tightened. As she tried to wriggle, a tingling warmth began in her head. There was a strange weakness to her limbs. Her hands grew heavy, helpless. He raised a syringe and raked it across her cheek, its malicious contents dripped from the tip of the needle. "You're stubborn like your sister. And for all your righteous living, now you're gonna die just like she did."

***

Keaton stomped the accelerator to the floor. He'd left work with the premonition something wasn't right. The closer he drew to Lindsey's house, the stronger it became. His reckless driving had already scared two vehicles to the side of the road. He rounded a curve and slammed on his brakes. Gravel pinged against the tail-gate.

Jack was leading his siblings across the yard to someone's house. Where were his cousins? Where were Lindsey and Lucy? Keaton jumped from his Bronco. Jack and Elizabeth both spoke at once. "Clayton's got Mom."

A woman stood in the open door-way of the house. She ushered the children inside and waved him on. Keaton jumped back inside and peeled gravel as he raced down the road. His heart beat a rhythm too fast to count.

Lindsey's house came into view. Following a gut feeling, Keaton bypassed her driveway and drove into the yard. Just as he expected, the back door stood wide open. Muted sounds could be heard over the beating of his heart. Keaton's blood boiled with anger. His thoughts wouldn't allow him to think of what Clayton might be doing.

Without thought of what awaited him, he raced through the door. Like a savage animal, Clayton pounced from the kitchen swinging a butcher's blade. His awkward movements were no match for Keaton's prowess. He angled to the side to miss the swipe of the blade and caught Clayton by the arm. Twisting it to its limit, he flung him into the wall with all his force.

Clayton's weaker build crumpled under the strength of Keaton's solid frame. The coward cried out in pain, but his eyes flared hatred as he tried to turn into Keaton. Keaton whipped him around and pummeled him in the gut. An animalistic desire tempted him to continue, but he knew it was an unfair fight.

He threw him to the ground and secured his arms with the addict's own belt. Clayton coughed and sputtered while Keaton turned to find Lindsey.

She lay on the kitchen floor, her skin so pale it appeared blue. An open syringe lay beside her. "God, no!"

Keaton fell to his knees and repeated the only prayer his lips could form. "God, no." His fingers shook uncontrollably. He couldn't find her pulse.

What could he do? Had she been injected with a drug? Keaton tilted back her head to administer CPR. As he bent closer his vision fell to the syringe one last time. It was still full.

Lindsey's head moved against his hand. Finally, she gasped.

Moments later, Keaton held Lindsey against his chest as they sat outside the ambulance and watched two officers dragged him toward their patrol car. Keaton had interrupted him before he could overdose her. Moments later, and he might've been too late.

He shuddered at the thought and pulled her closer. Clayton's offensive smell left a trail behind him as the police dragged him to their car.

Lindsey sniffed and cleared her throat. "I should have run, but I didn't know the children had already gotten away. Why didn't I grab a knife before he walked through the door?"

"Shh," Keaton's tried to soothe her but a tremor claimed his voice. His heart still kept an exhaustive beat. They'd almost lost what they hadn't even begun.

Officer Cooper stopped in front of them. "Now we know why he never left any finger prints. He doesn't have any. He probably burned them off with battery acid." He cleared his throat. "But we've got him now and he's not going anywhere."

Neither he nor Lindsey replied. Fear still held them captive. He stared across the yard and into the forest that bordered her property. He never wanted her living here again.

She straightened and met Keaton's eyes. "It's weird. I keep thinking of all the things I should've done and the only thing I did do was repeat a verse over and over in my mind."

Keaton smoothed her hair away from her eyes. "What was the verse?"

"Isaiah 41:10. Fear thou not; for I am with thee: be not dismayed; for I am thy God: I will strengthen thee; yea, I will help thee; yea, I will uphold thee with the right hand of my righteousness."

Keaton slowly nodded. "And He did."

***

"Are you game for doing something different?"

Lindsey ran her hand over her head and through her hair. Yesterday's trauma still haunted her. "Definitely, we could all use a break from, from . . ."

Keaton understood her reluctance to give words to all they'd endured. To help her avoid the awful thought, he moved the conversation forward. "The Butterfly House has a special event this weekend. We could dress up and tour the atrium, attend the event, then go out to dinner."

Happiness danced in her eyes. "Oh, Keaton, that sounds wonderful. But," her eyes dimmed, "that would be so costly."

A smile tugged at the corner of his mouth. She was so pure and sweet. Such a trustworthy woman, he vowed in his heart to always respect her. "Lindsey, I can afford it, don't worry." He could also afford many more fun days spent with the family.

He took her hand in his and pulled her to him. "And in case you need something new to wear, Lucy would love an excuse to go shopping."

"Oh, I couldn't. Really, Keaton, just getting a day away is treat enough for me."'

"Maybe I wasn't entirely thinking of you."

She cocked her head to the side and smiled. "What do you mean?"

"I saw some pretty dresses in the window of the store in town. I sure wouldn't mind seeing you in one of them." He'd prepared himself for her denial, knowing she wouldn't feel comfortable accepting a gift. "And besides pleasing me, you'd be doing this for my sister. She doesn't have reason to shop anymore, but it would make her day."

She sighed, "I don't know . . ."

He gave her a pleading look and added, "I'd feel better if you weren't sitting around tomorrow dwelling on everything. Mom will watch the kids. Run to town with Lucy, and have a little fun."

He knew she was only agreeing to please him. She bit her lip and looked away before responding. "Okay."

"Good. And don't forget to buy a dress. If you don't, Lucy won't, and that's half the fun."

"Keaton, I–"

"You have the money." He handed her a sealed card. "It's my gift to you." He bent his head to hers and kissed her lips. The familiar longing that came every time he touched her sent his heart to pounding. He couldn't wait for the day she was his. That day was coming, as long as everything went as planned.

***

"How about this one?" Lucy held up a cotton sundress.

"Nah, I can't wear yellow, it washes me out."

"Good, because I can." Lucy smiled and bounced to the dressing rooms.

Lindsey flipped through a rack of dresses, but her eyes kept pulling back to the dress on a mannequin in the window.

Lucy stepped from the dressing room and twirled. "What do you think?"

"Oh, Lucy, that dress looks great on you. You're a ray of sunshine."

Lucy paraded around the mirror smiling. "I'm going to buy it. It's been so long since I dressed in something that made me feel pretty. Thank you, Lindsey, for asking me to come with you." Her eyes met Lindsey's through the reflection of the mirror. "Now it's your turn."

"Oh, I don't know. I really don't need a new–"

"Don't give me that. My brother gave you money and yes, you do need a new dress, I've seen your closet." Both girls laughed and Lucy shoved her inside her dressing room.

Within a few moments, Lucy flung a dress over the top of the door. "Try this green one on first. I want to see it."

Lindsey bit her lip. The dress hadn't appealed to her on the rack. She shrugged into it and opened the door. "I don't like it."

Lucy's eyes squinted in consideration. "You're right. It doesn't fit your personality. Here, try this blue one."

Lindsey shook her head. "Okay, Easter bunny."

A giggle sounded from the other side of the door. "Can I help it if I like pastels?"

Lindsey stood in the mirror, wrapped in blue. It was pretty, but it still didn't grab her the way she thought the one from the window would. She opened the door and walked past Lucy. "Let me guess, you have another one. Is it lavender?"

Lucy hid a dress behind her. With an innocent look, she shrugged her shoulders. "Maybe."

Lindsey came back dragging the mannequin. "Here, help me get this off." They giggled and snuck the plastered form into a dressing room.

Finally, she opened the door wearing the dress that had originally caught her eye. White eyelet cotton overlaid a glimmer of bold pink satin. Gathered at the waist, it gently billowed right below the knee.

"Wow. Lindsey, my brother is going to love you in that."

***

Keaton fastened the buttons of his white shirt and tucked it into his slacks. He hoped his change from his usual attire of jeans and T-shirt didn't give away his surprise. Lindsey hadn't asked what the special event would be. She seemed pleased enough just to get away.

He winked at his folks before stepping through the door. They had their work cut out for them. A clear, blue sky welcomed his cheery mood as he crossed the road. With Clayton's arrest, Keaton was free to secure his future with Lindsey. The addict had confessed to over-dosing Lauren during his tirade in the patrol car, which meant he'd be put away for a long, long time.

Elizabeth and Samantha met him at the door in their regular Sunday dresses. Like their mother, none of the children knew what to expect.

Lindsey stepped from the kitchen, her arms full of drinks and snacks for the trip, but even that couldn't hide how beautiful she looked.

Keaton paused mid-stride with his jaw hung open. "You are beautiful."

She dropped her gaze to the load in her arms to hide her embarrassment. "I take it you like the dress?"

Keaton couldn't pull his eyes away. The dress fit her perfectly, in shape and personality. He gathered his senses and helped her with the load in her arms. He wanted to tell her everything, but he couldn't. He'd worked too hard to plan this surprise. He settled for what he always felt. "I love you."

A couple hours later he pulled into the parking lot of the atrium. The children's enthusiasm hadn't paled with the drive, if anything, it had increased. Lindsey tried to quiet them and finally shrugged her shoulders. "Sorry, Mike never took them anywhere, so they're overly excited."

His thoughts sped ahead for the next year. If they never went anywhere, then he'd need to take them to the zoo and Grant's Farm and—

"Can we get out?"

Their voices brought him back to the present. "You bet!"

After pulling the children away from the gift shop, they stepped through the double doors into a different world. Butterflies danced in the air, flitting between plants with bright leaves and flowers ranging from philodendron to golden trumpet, peace lilies, and more. The foliage crowded the walkways and climbed the walls.

Exotic, fragile wings of every color fluttered around them. Lindsey pointed to a bench where white wings of lace graced an elderly woman's knee. The woman smiled, "This is called a Paper Kite. Of course, I think the name Queen Anne's Lace would have been better suited."

Keaton glanced to a hanging feeder filled with slices of banana. Two brown butterflies shared a piece of fruit. "They aren't very pretty."

Lindsey leaned forward. "Take a closer look."

Keaton peered with her. Bright blue hid inside their folded wings waiting to explode with color as they opened wide in flight. Keaton directed Lindsey's attention to something else as he checked on the children. His sister stood by the door and nodded his way before disappearing. Everything was going as planned.

It didn't take long for Lindsey to miss the kids. Almost as soon as the door closed behind Lucy, she turned in search of them. Concern filled her voice. "Keaton, where are the children?"

"I sent them on a special errand. They'll be okay."

Lindsey's eyes widened before she set her jaw. Keaton smiled gently, he'd upset the mama bear in her. "Do you trust me?"

Her features softened as she stared into the depths of his eyes. "Yes, I do."

"Good. Then relax and practice repeating that phrase."

She quirked an eyebrow at him before shaking her head. She had no idea what was going on, just as he'd planned.

Keaton cleared his throat. "Lucy told me you'd mentioned wanting a fairy tale. What did you mean?"

She turned her head away. "Your sister evidently talks too much."

"Don't be upset. I wanted to know what your dreams were. I want them to be mine, as well."

Lindsey swallowed and stared at him. Moisture glistened in her eyes. It was so easy to touch her heart.

Keaton took her hand and led her down a path. "Lindsey,"

Eyes of chocolate met his with a hopeful yearning. "Yes, Keaton."

"I'd like to give you that fairy tale." He directed her to look beside her. She turned in time to see Elizabeth emerge dressed as Cinderella.

Lindsey threw a hand to her mouth and cried, "Oh!"

From another path came Josh as Peter Pan. Lindsey giggled as the rest of her children appeared dressed in various fairy tale costumes. Tears slid from her eyes as she turned back to Keaton. "Thank you." She shook her head. "How did you do it?"

"Before I answer that, I have a question for you." He bent to one knee and withdrew a box from his pocket. He flipped open the top to reveal a princess cut diamond ring.

"Oh, Keaton," she whispered.

"Will you marry me, Princess?"

Lindsey's pastor stepped in front of them and smiled.

She gasped. "Yes!"

Keaton's parents and sister moved to stand beside them for the ceremony. Lindsey's eyes widened in complete surprise.

She turned back to him and spoke for his ears only. "You're incredible. My very own Prince Charming!"

A Note from the Author

Thankfully rural America still exists. In select parts of the country, it's not unusual to see the bed of an old pickup truck filled with smiling faces heading down a gravel road to the river. Or have someone stop by your house with a casserole when life throws an unexpected curve or just because you're new in town. I'm thankful for living this type of life. It moves at a slower pace and makes for great story-telling.

Thank you for reading Coveted Bride. If you're someone who lives with the scars of emotional abuse, I hope this story has shown how to regain your confidence and enjoy all the blessings God has in store for you.

Through this story I also wanted to convey how important it is to safe-guard our children in today's world. My mother had a code word for us growing up. I've never forgotten it and thought it a worthy enough idea to pass on. Protect your children by educating them of the evils of this world. Make sure they know what to do when in trouble. And lastly, pray for them.

I enjoy hearing from my readers and can be found at http://www.reginatittel.blogspot.com, or you can leave me a message at reginatittel@gmail.com.

Also, if you enjoyed Coveted Bride, please consider leaving a review at amazon.com, barnesandnoble.com, or smashwords.com. Your encouraging words could be the catalyst someone else needs to purchase this book. Not only would you be sharing the Godly messages I shared with you, but you would also help promote me as an author.

Thanks again, and God bless!

Regina

Resources to learn more:

http://EzineArticles.com/1459954

www.avpublications.com

New Age Bible Versions by Gail Riplinger

www.counselingcenter.illinois.edu/?page_id=168

Cherished Stranger

The Ozark Durham Series Vol. 4

by

Regina Tittel

Lucy Durham Watson lost track of her sponsor child during Romania's flood. Now that the Christian organization has located her again, she's not about to lose her a second time. Disregarding advice from her family, she helps Anika and her father gain U.S. citizenship to live on her farm.

Life in Romania's poverty is a stark contrast to the comforts of the Ozarks. A fact proven by Dorin, the father of her sponsor child. Governed by his pride and his disapproval of Lucy's spontaneous and often reckless personality, they clash from the start.

But when Lucy becomes the target of a stalker, everything changes.

Coming Soon

Have <u>The Ozark Durham Series</u> sent to your home!

Item	Qty.	Price Ea.	Total
Abandoned Hearts		$ 11.95	
Unexpected Kiss		$ 11.95	
Coveted Bride		$ 11.95	
Cherished Stranger		$ 11.95	
Merchandise Total			
$3.99 s/h			
MO Residents add 5.85% tax			
Order Total			

Name   (Please Print)

Address

City   State   Zip

Signature (if under 18, a parent or guardian must sign)

☐ Please contact me to discuss a discounted purchase for use in a youth group, book club, or other related service where five or more books are needed.

Make Check Payable to:

Regina Tittel

Rt. 1 Box 1795

Patton MO 63662

Coveted Bride